We the Peeps

A Political Caper and Wish Fulfillment

BY

MORGAN HUNT

Although the author has taken pains to give this work an underpinning of verisimilitude, it is a work of fiction. Public figures who appear in the text by name do so entirely without their knowledge or cooperation, and any statements by them or actions taken by them derive solely from the author's imagination, and the other characters and events described are also wholly imaginary. Any resemblance to non-public figures or to real events is coincidental.

For Chaya Rivka

ACKNOWLEDGEMENTS

I gratefully acknowledge my Alpha and Beta Readers: Tamar Berg, Fran Brass, M.J. Daspit, Nancie Furgang, Len Kornblau, Patricia McGraw, Robin McSky, Sheila Melzer, Linda Pollack, Sylvia Saxon, Angela Shelton, Terry and Fred Sylvanus, Maggie Thompson, and Lucy Warren who read early drafts and provided feedback so that this book could find its way; and to Rosalind Leighton, who not only read chapter by chapter and provided feedback but also copy-edited with a meticulous eye.

Special appreciation goes to artist Sally Montiano for her wonderful cover design and graphics; to Charles Douglas of Rogue Valley Television in Ashland, Oregon for technical info; to medical student Kysa McSky for info on DeVille's injury; to J.D. Hunt, FAA Automation Engineering Manager, for technical info on flight; to attorneys Barbara Cohen of Oakland, CA and Linda Pollack of Novato, CA for guidance on legal topics; to my son Jeffrey V. Hunt, for help with Spanish translation, and to Edie Reba Murphy who was an Alpha reader, brainstormer, provider of a writing sanctuary, photographer for my cover photo, and who personified encouragement.

"A can-do country has been saddled with a
do-nothing political system."
-Fahreed Zakaria

"A little rebellion now and then is a good
thing."
-Thomas Jefferson

LIST OF MAIN CHARACTERS

White House

Basho Samuels Peabody, US President

Roger Shellish, White House Chief of Staff

Sarantha Peabody, President's daughter

Demetra Phillips, President's ex-fiancée; a physician
with Doctors Without Borders

Peeps

Raven Ferrera, TV Reporter

Navya Ghazal, VP of Sales for commercial real estate

Emery Palmer, Prison chaplain

Glenda Tramboy, Community college history instructor

Ted McGregor, Auto mechanic

Vivi Huarochiri, High school student; hacker

DeVille Tiamante, Wounded Vietnam veteran; chef

Part I: Paul Revere's Ride

Chapter 1

Late Aug. 201X

As morning sunlight streamed into the Oval Office, the President stared at the marine blue diary atop the Resolute desk. The cover had faded and it smelled of mildew. He turned to an entry in the journal made about 20 years ago. A third of the way down the page, a paragraph caught his eye.

As we climbed up to the tree house, I could feel the heat of his cock pressing against me. When we got inside, he turned me to face him, grabbed me in his arms and pulled me up against him. I could feel every part of him, all of his strength....we are so mad for one another! I pulled his shirt off and he began to do that nuzzly kissing on my neck that always turns me on. When he entered me I gave him a welcome squeeze. We made long and leisurely love. Oh god, his smell... that blend of his aftershave, his sweat, even his semen… Damn, did I really write that? Tonight we ourselves were the shooting stars.

His pulse did a syncopated Skip to My Lou. That might've been the best sex of my life, he thought, suppressing a grin. The President took a deep breath, and summoned a Secret Service agent. "Firth, I need you to locate Senator Lacomb and bring him to the Oval Office. To me, personally. He'll probably be in his Senate office. And I need you to find his daughter, Angela Lacomb, and bring her here, too. Delegate if you want to, but I need to see both the Senator and his daughter ASAP. It's a matter of national security."

The agent, a veteran of two administrations, sensed the President's urgency and hurried out the door.

Moments later in the bathroom off the Oval Office, a sandy-haired, blue-eyed Hiawatha reflected from the mirror back into the face of President Basho Samuels Peabody. As his second campaign manager had once remarked, 'What Anglo could resist the urge to vote for a guy who looks like Robert Redford with Geronimo's cheekbones?' His *first* campaign manager had dared to ask, 'What the hell kind of name is Basho'?

Peabody and the media were well aware that his party had nominated him out of desperation. Two strong candidates were deepening a party rift and splitting delegates, sapping GOP chances for an electoral win. The Party Chair, the one with the name that sounds so elite it might have been extracted from a royal anus with sugar tongs, asked him if he'd be willing to leave his post as Director of the Better Living Through Enterprise think tank to run for President.

"Haven't you vetted me? I'm a bachelor. I have a teenage daughter whose mother I never married. And my daughter's on a first-name basis with her truant officer. If you think you have controversy now…"

"Peabody, we need you. Popeye and Sasquatch are ruining this party!" Popeye was the Party Chair's nickname for the GOP's weak-tea establishment golden boy, and Sasquatch was what he called billionaire celebrity mogul Hrump. "We'll slip you in at the convention; catch the two of them off guard."

"Right. Who's going to nominate me?"

"Sue Miyamoto, delegate from Hawaii."

"Hawaii – one of our party's strongest outposts," Peabody needled.

"I've already talked to her. She'll do it."

"You spoke to her before you talked to me?"

"I understand the game."

"I understand the game, too. If I accept the nomination, I pick my own V.P." Peabody knew the Party Chair wanted Senator Henry Lacomb, a good ole boy who never met a lobbyist whose butt he wouldn't kiss.

The Party Chair caved. Peabody knew he was not the best person in the nation to sit in the Oval Office. He also knew he wasn't the worst. After a night of soul-searching aided by Royal Lochnagar Scotch, he accepted his party's nomination. He chose Athena Storm, an ex-New England Senator, Iraq War veteran and nurse to run as his Vice President. She was an *ex*-Senator because she believed in compromise and moderation. Peabody knew that even if he screwed things up, she'd be able to unscrew them. He couldn't say that about most people in Washington. And so he had begun his luge ride through the cesspool of American politics. He'd first sniffed that cesspool when he'd run for Congress from his home district in Wisconsin. Two terms in the House of Representatives had more than satisfied his curiosity.

Sensing he had neither horrific ambition nor hubris, the Beltway media hadn't taken his candidacy seriously. His fundraising efforts and poll results had been, to put it kindly, insignificant -- until two weeks before Election Day. On that chill morning, a snide politico wanted to interview him about his Native American heritage. "Mr. Peabody, let's begin by covering what is now familiar territory. Your first name, Basho, is not Native American, right?"

"That's correct. I was named after a Japanese poet. My mother adored Asian cultural arts." His mother felt her ancestors lost something culturally when they migrated from Asia, rather like moving from the Upper East side to Staten Island.

The reporter took it up a notch. "Your ancestors are Algonquians from the Ojibwa Tribe, correct?"

"My maternal grandmother's ancestors, yes." Where's he going with this? he wondered. His Ojibwa ancestors were a people known for canoes and wild rice; hardly controversial. But Peabody could smell the reporter leading up to something.

"Didn't the Ojibwa declare war on the State of Wisconsin in 1959?"

Peabody stared at him.

10

The interviewer gleamed with gotcha. "In your opinion, is it appropriate for someone with such an anti-U.S., perhaps even treasonous, heritage to hold the highest office in the land?"

There, in front of a national TV audience, Basho Samuels Peabody snapped back: "Bite me! A small group – one tribal council – declared a non-violent war on Wisconsin over broken treaties about fishing rights. A *non-violent* war. In 1959, three years before I was born!" Peabody sized the guy up. "Perhaps you think we should exclude from presidential candidacy anyone whose ancestors are British; we were once at war with them, too. You may have heard of it… a little thing called the American Revolution?"

Voters swooned. Dubbed the Bite Me Boy by the frenzied media, his polls surged. Like Sasquatch, he had the backbone to put the media in its place and the testosterone to balance the Democrats' estrogen. Like Popeye, he looked the role and could think on his feet. Basho Samuels Peabody was elected President of the United States with 53% of the vote.

That was twenty-one months ago and it had been downhill ever since. What Peabody suspected before his party's recruitment call was true: the American people were bifurcated, pissed off, and in no mood for the artifice and soullessness of politics as usual. Once in office, the Party tried to control him, but Peabody was no one's puppet. With riots on the streets of America almost every week, probably the only reason he hadn't been assassinated was that he was essentially honest with the American people. He didn't always tell them what they wanted to hear, but he told the truth. Often, anyway.

11

Peabody decided his fair-haired Hiawatha visage was sufficiently groomed for the day ahead.

Senator Henry Lacomb slumped over the 514-page energy bill the chamber would soon vote on for final approval before sending it to the White House. His $2200 designer eyeglasses didn't slip down his nose like the old pair used to. Nice to know a few grand could solve that problem. As Chair of the Energy and Natural Resources Committee, he saw no reason not to savor the fact that oil and gas lobbyists were a generous sort.

So far, the bill looked fine. They'd incorporated the trade-offs and tweaks agreed upon in the Conference Committee; he'd checked those immediately. Now he was skimming page by page. The full text of the bill had been problematic. For reasons that remained fuzzy, whole paragraphs had disappeared. One time several pages belonging to an entirely different bill had been integrated into the document. He knew no one in the House had bothered to read the bill line by line, so he wanted to eyeball it himself before it went for final Senate vote. He wanted no room for error when it was sent to Peabody for signature. That sorry excuse, that RINO, that contemptible sea slug …

Secret Service Agent Firth startled the senator when he touched his elbow. "Senator, the President requests that you see him in the Oval Office immediately."

"I am a U. S. Senator, for god sakes," huffed Lacomb, "not some school boy to be summoned to the principal's office. This bill is going for final vote today. I need to…"

Agent Firth whispered in the senator's ear. "I don't mean to upset you, sir, but when the President of the United States needs to see you, you go." He accompanied his words with an upward pressure on the senator's arm, lifting Lacomb from his seat.

Senator Lacomb had read through the bill's first 402 pages. He sighed, texted one of his aides: *Called 2 White House on urgent matter. Energy Bill looks gd 2 me. Lets ram this thru!*, and followed Agent Firth out the door. How long will this new annoyance from Peabody take, he wondered. The Senate votes on the bill in less than an hour.

The President returned from the bathroom to the Oval Office, nearly colliding with Roger Shellish, his Chief of Staff. Roger was one of the few human beings in D.C. whom Peabody trusted. When Peabody was a 32-year-old freshman Representative, he had stopped for java at the same café each morning. And every morning he was served by the same barista, a 23-year-old student from DeKalb, Illinois working his way through Georgetown Law School. One day Peabody left his wallet on the counter, and the carrot-top barista biked two blocks down D Street to return it to him. From his spiky red hair to his occasionally mismatched socks, Roger Shellish made Peabody feel as though the gates of his administration were protected by an honest jester with an international law degree. Somehow that seemed appropriate.

"Good morning, Mr. President. Agent Firth requests time in your schedule for a meeting with Senator Lacomb. I don't see Lacomb on your sched…"

"I know, Roger. Cancel whatever; I need to meet with the senator immediately. Need to see his daughter, too. Expect she'll arrive later."

"Sir, may I ask what this is about?"

Peabody picked up the diary again. "It's about this, Roger. If I read parts of it to you, you'd get a hard-on and I'd hate to feel responsible for that." The President's response made his Chief of Staff blush. "I look forward to dealing with the Lacombs with all the enthusiasm I reserve for my annual colonoscopy. I wish I could have you right at my side. But this matter is something I have to handle myself."

"How can I help?"

"Clear my schedule for at least an hour and get Lacomb in here. Make whatever excuses you want; I trust your judgment." He took a breath; felt the cardiac polka again. "And please get Demetra Phillips on a secure line. I've tried her four times already and can't reach her."

The Chief of Staff exited; moments later, Lacomb was ushered in. His mood hovered between curious, peeved and wary. "What can I do for you, Mr. President?"

Peabody gestured toward a chair. Lacomb sat. Peabody picked up the diary and waved it in the air. "Recognize this?"

"No. Should I?"

Peabody knew Lacomb was a weasel, but had hoped the Oval Office setting might stir a vestige of patriotism.

"Angela Lacomb is your daughter, right?"

"You know she is."

"And she writes the Beltway Boogie blog?"

"Yes, but I don't see what …"

"You don't see? Well, here. Take a good look!" President Peabody held the diary up so Lacomb could see it and flipped its pages. "This was delivered by special courier this morning. The accompanying note said that your daughter had photocopied every page and would run excerpts from it in her blog, starting tomorrow."

"What is it? Your kid's diary?"

"My ex-fiancée's diary, a diary she kept the first two years she and I were together."

The furrows on Lacomb's brow cleared. He licked his lips. "Something juicy in there?"

"Yes, and from what I can see, you're in dire need of learning the techniques mentioned on these pages." He retracted his acerbic humor and got down to business. "My daughter and her mother could be damaged by this."

"I see; yes; might even put some dings in your own shiny armor."

"Damn it to hell, Henry. Where's your sense of decency?"

"You think I had something to do with this?" Lacomb objected. "Come on; this is Watergate plumber-level crap. If I wanted to.."

President Peabody looked at Lacomb. "If you wanted to, you'd what?" Peabody held the gaze until Lacomb looked down. "If you had nothing to do with this, then why is your daughter threatening to publish these diary

15

excerpts on her blog? Why would she want to embarrass me, my ex, or my daughter?"

Senator Lacomb was speechless, a rare occurrence.

The President's intercom buzzed; he answered. After listening, he told Lacomb, "The Secret Service has located your daughter. We'll see if she understands the trouble she's in."

The President buzzed his secretary. "Have coffee and a sandwich sent up for Senator Lacomb. He's going to be here a while."

Two minutes later Roger announced an incoming call from Dr. Demetra Phillips. The President took the call in his private office. "Demetra!"

"Is Sarantha OK?" The static on the line sounded like the Tin Man shaving Brillo stubble.

"She's fine. Where the hell are you, anyway?"

"I'm working at Mbera Camp. In Mauritania." A pause; more static. "What's going on, Sam? They pulled me out of surgery for your call."

"Remember that diary you kept when we were dating? A Beltway blogger got her hands on it. Some of what you wrote could be considered, er, salacious. The blogger is Senator Lacomb's daughter. She's threatening to publish parts of your diary on her blog."

"I disposed of that journal years ago when you announced your candidacy; tossed it in the trash. Whatever diary this blogger has is a fake."

"Are you sure, hon? It looks like your handwriting."

"Maybe she's a good forger."

President Basho Peabody squirmed in his leather chair. His voice grew quieter. "Demmy, remember what we did at two in the morning in that playground in Prague? Remember?" He paused to let the memory revive. "Or where I'm most ticklish?" Peabody heard her chuckle softly in response. "Remember that move I learned that could make you come over and over again? All of that's in this journal."

Peabody's voice had softened but Demetra's hardened. "I have no idea how or why things happen the way they do in Washington." She paused. Static bristled over the connection. "Tell Sarantha I'll be back in the states for Christmas."

"I will. Demmy, you're 100% sure you destroyed that diary?"

"Positive."

"OK, thanks. I know what you're doing is important, so I'll let you get back to it. Love you."

"Love you, too."

There was always love between them. But how could love ever surmount the priorities of Doctors Without Borders? When he had proposed, she'd specified in detail how many lives would not be saved if she didn't travel abroad and dedicate her life to healing. How do you argue with that? If he knew, maybe he wouldn't be 4000 miles from the only woman he'd ever loved, the mother of his child.

President Peabody disconnected the call. He stared again at the diary and scrutinized the handwriting once more. It did look like Demetra's but maybe, hmm…. How could the writer of a forged diary know such intimate details?

The strangest thing about the entire incident, Peabody considered, was that I fully intended to sign Lacomb's energy bill. Why did he think I would balk? We don't see eye to eye on everything, but on energy, we mostly agree. The economy needs an ongoing supply of gas and oil, supplemented by green energy. Why would Lacomb put his blogger daughter up to such a thing? What was the agenda? What was the pay-off?

After he'd kept Lacomb cooling his heels for a while, Peabody called him back into the Oval Office. Against protocol, the senator spoke first. "I hope you're satisfied. I missed the vote on my energy bill because of this."

"You think I should sit back and allow your daughter to threaten the President of the United States with blackmail?"

"Of course not."

The President received a text message and read it. He looked up. "Senator, your bill passed the House and the Senate and is on its way here for signature. I intend to sign it. The Secret Service and I will have a little chat with your daughter. I don't know what this is all about, but you and your daughter had better not harm me or my daughter. Or anyone else we love." With a curt nod, he dismissed Lacomb.

Later Roger Shellish brought the new Energy Bill to Peabody's desk for signature. "The press corps is waiting for a photo op when you sign it," Roger said.

"That's scheduled for 2:15, right?"

"Yes…"

Something in Roger's voice made Peabody wonder. "What is it?"

"I think there may be a few typos in the bill."

"Well, that's not the end of the world. What kind of typos are we talking about?"

"The new energy bill sets aside a generous amount of funding for fricking."

President Peabody laughed. "You mean fracking."

"No," said Roger. "I mean fricking."

Chapter 2

A Few Months Earlier

"*Ancee Gazoxfrrhn, please meet your passajur at gate smooo-tiddy-oo. Ancee Gazoxfrrhn, please meet your passajur at gate smooo-tiddy-oo.*"

Raven Ferrera watched a teen in line ahead of her at Logan International Airport surrender his iPod and ear buds to the conveyor belt. She located her compact at the bottom of her purse and highlighted the bronze of her cheekbones. She tried various facial expressions in the compact mirror. If she looked too calm, they'd suspect something. Too fidgety wouldn't work either. Ordinary apprehension was the ticket. She'd draw on her own experience. After all, she'd gone through airport security dozens of times when she *wasn't* carrying a concealed weapon.

As Raven passed through the high tech Gates of Hades, all hell did, indeed, break loose. The x-ray image of a pistol-shaped metal object guaranteed a fuss. But her carry-on bag with its plastic explosives slipped serenely along the conveyor belt past the scanner.

Two large Security staffers, a man with a gun on his hip and an intimidating armed matron, swooped in on Raven and handcuffed her before she could exhale. Murmurs and gasps galvanized the security area. In a microsecond this was no longer another boring queue.

Raven turned to see if her cameraman had recorded their ploy. He gave her a thumbs-up. She'd done it! She'd done it! Raven had a hard time maintaining a somber face for Security. "Call Thomas!" she yelled to the videographer as more armed personnel maneuvered her into a private room. The male guard departed.

"Ms., er, Gaston," Raven scrutinized the matron's ID badge. "I'm a reporter for KCUP-TV in LA. I'm doing an exposé on airport security. Take off the handcuffs and I'll show you my credentials."

The matron's expression did not change, which was just as well since Raven suddenly remembered her credentials were in her purse, still on the security conveyor belt. She'd meant to transfer them from her purse to her slacks pocket. Oops. She tried a different tactic. "Look, in my carry-on there's a jewelry box. Underneath its lining are plastic explosives. But don't worry – there's no detonator. I'm not trying to hurt anyone."

The TSA matron listened to Raven, then placed a call on some kind of walkie talkie. It sounded to Raven like, *"Oh-one-niner, retro set zebra four four. Resin sebellious. Resin sebellious. Over."* Raven had no trouble interpreting the matron's next command.

"Sit down. I'm going to remove your blouse."

Raven sat.

The matron's fingers, which last evening blotted a winning card at Bingo, manipulated the buttons of Raven's designer silk blouse. Raven had splurged on Rodeo Drive because she knew she'd be on camera for this segment. The indignity of being partially undressed off camera was a small price to pay for such a professional coup.

21

When the matron opened Raven's blouse, the pistol-shaped lighter tucked into her bra came into view. Wordlessly, the TSA matron retrieved the trinket from Raven's modest cleavage and examined it.

Raven tried again. "As you can see, the gun is a cigarette lighter. We wanted to see if setting off the walk-through alarm would distract the screeners at the conveyor belt. And it did. They let the plastic explosives through the …"

The door flew open and two more women entered the room– one in a business suit, the other in a TSA uniform. This one carried Raven's blue overnight case and her purse. When Mrs. Gaston showed the cigarette lighter pistol to the women, someone snickered. Through whispered hisses, Raven heard the words "TV" and "reporter." The woman in the business suit told Gaston to remove Raven's handcuffs.

"Can I button my blouse?" Raven asked no one in particular. No one in particular answered. She buttoned her blouse.

The TSA uniformed woman opened the blue overnight case and retrieved the jewelry box, lifting it with utmost caution.

"There's no detonator," Raven reminded them.

Moments later a soldier wearing Bomb Squad insignia entered the room and with a nod, removed the jewelry box to parts unknown. After a lot of folderol the woman in the business suit returned Raven's purse and cell phone to her. "I'm Andrea Tarmini, Logan International Airport's Security Liaison. This may be just a story to KCUP, but it's a serious matter to us. Do you understand?"

Raven nodded. "Our attorneys coordinated this with the TSA Administrator in Washington. It was approved as an exercise."

This infuriated Ms. Tarmini. "You will be escorted into our Security Holding Area where you will await further instructions." With a crisp nod to Mrs. Gaston, she and her sidekick departed.

Gaston escorted Raven down a hall off the main terminal. They reached a reinforced door with a solitary window pane crisscrossed with wire. No sign or label identified the door or the room beyond it. Gaston swiped a card to unlock the door and offered Raven a little shove. "Wait here." Raven heard the door's locking mechanism engage as Gaston departed.

Inside the room stood a National Guardsman with a rifle in his hands and a shaving nick along his jaw line. The Guardsman addressed her in a heartland drawl. "Ma'am, I'm Lance Corporal Walters; I'm in charge of this Holding Area. Rest rooms are over there." He tilted the tip of his rifle toward one wall. "Water cooler, soda and snack machines, there. You can use your phone, but all calls within this area are monitored, Ma'am." The private snapped back to attention near the door and let Raven get acquainted with her surroundings.

Raven's eyes went to the video cameras in all corners of the room. Big Brother was on red alert. The only window in the entire room was the small one in the door. An overhead TV monitor blared CNN. Three rows of beige plastic chairs offered seats, if not a warm welcome.

Raven felt like an adrenaline sparkle-cluster. She'd been pushing her producer for this opportunity for four years. She had to tell someone! She looked around at her fellow travelers. What kind of people would be in the airport's Security Holding Area? If she'd given it much thought before the KCUP-TV exploit (she hadn't), she'd have imagined glum young men with beards and the emotional equanimity of Ted Nugent. Or maybe the odd conspiracy theorist. Yet the people in this holding area looked disappointingly ordinary.

A stocky woman of East Indian ethnicity chain-popped chocolate-covered cherries and watched CNN. Her clothes were expensive, her manicure perfect, her demeanor confident. I'll bet she's a Bollywood exec, guessed Raven. Should I recognize her?

In the back row of chairs sat a man who looked to be in his 40s with silver streaks in wavy black hair and a noticeable 5 o'clock shadow. His attention was focused on the book he was reading, *Sin and Grace in Christian Counseling.*

To Lance Corporal Walters' left paced a handsome guy who looked like some Norman Rockwell farmer who grows tractors from seed. What was that dawg doing in a Security holding room?

A spitfire Latina in baggy camo who appeared too young –16? --to be detained without adult supervision circled the room. She circled the room, talking incessantly on her cell, not caring whether Big Brother listened in. Big Brother's Spanish skills would have to be *maravilloso* to follow the conversation but her F-U body language was easy to translate.

A slender Boomer-aged woman leaned forward, engrossed in TV news. Her youthful haircut was attractive but her thick eyebrows begged for tweezers and a sedative. They curled in different directions, as though they couldn't decide whether to remain on her face or to seek asylum.

"Attention passajurs. Macadamian Airlines Flight three nine four to Torunto hash been cancelled. Passajurs holding tickets, please consult yer airlines representzzzhif. Fenk you."

Raven approached the Boomer woman, feigning interest in CNN for a few minutes. When she could no longer contain herself, she announced, "We're going to be on the news tomorrow!"

The bushy-browed woman introduced herself. "My name's Glenda. What do you mean, 'we're going to be on the news?' "

Raven smiled as she shook Glenda's hand. "Raven Ferrera. I'm a reporter with KCUP-TV in L.A.. We came up with a security exercise that fooled the airport's TSA workers. My video guy got it all. It'll be picked up by every major news station tomorrow."

"Ferrera? Are you part Spanish? Italian?" a curious Glenda inquired.

"Part Spanish, on my Dad's side. Also some Portuguese. African-American all the way back to the founding days of Charleston on my mom's side, " Raven shared.

"I'm a Heinz 57 mix. Some German and French, lots of Irish and English." Glenda seemed to have used up all of the social grace she could muster for the moment. Her next words had an angry bite to them. "Damned idiots! This country can't even fly planes on time any more. But it's a

25

real stretch even for these bozos to think that I'm a terrorist." Glenda gave Raven another look. "Aren't you worried? You've heard of the Patriot Act, with all of its abuses? The government could order a drone strike on this entire room. We'll be lucky if we ever see our homes again."

"That's a bit extreme." Raven's eyes roamed the room, seeking someone less agitated to converse with.

" 'The history of liberty is a history of resistance' – Woodrow Wilson."

"You a history buff?"

"I taught history at a community college."

The lanky Norman Rockwell type walked over. "Ted McGregor," he said, offering his hand to each of them. "May I join you?"

He had manners, all right, thought Raven, and a lean hard build that made him seem like the guy whose help she'd most want if she had a flat tire. But, she reminded herself, Timothy McVeigh had looked clean cut and all-American, too. Raven's experience told her that people with a sense of humor were rarely angry enough to be violent. With some trepidation she asked, "Pardon me for being cautious, but given the circumstances…" She gestured around the Holding Area. "Plan any hijacks lately?"

"A few hijinks maybe." His smile disarmed her. "You two look awful suspicious."

"Raven Ferrera, reporter for KCUP-TV. My station did an exposé on the security here and TSA's not too happy with me at the moment."

26

"I'm an auto mechanic, kind of a Lost in Transmission guy." He had a charming smile and knew how to use it. "I'm from Boulder; on my way back from a special training course on Jeep 4 by 4s."

Glenda appraised Ted. "Glenda Tramboy. I was on a tour of the Middle East; I cut my vacation short to fly back to see my mother. Her nursing home called me yesterday morning and told me she had a second heart attack. And now, this! I'm being detained because I happened to be in Egypt and Cyprus the same time there were terror incidents." She challenged him, "You haven't told us why you're here."

"I spilled coffee on my passport. They think I did it on purpose to disguise my identity." Ted eyed the clock on the wall. "I wonder how long this is going to take. A friend is picking me up at the airport."

"Why don't you call him?" Raven asked.

"They confiscated my phone."

Raven dug her cell from her purse. "Here, use mine."

"Thanks." Ted walked a few feet away and began dialing.

On TV a CNN talking head expressed the nation's frustration and weariness about the latest unarmed African American man shot dead by police. This time, in Boise.

The Holding Area door opened again and a 6′4″, 315-pound sirocco of disruption blew in. The new arrival had russet-colored skin, a well muscled frame, and an uneven scar within thick gray hair. "You can't do this! I know my rights!" He expressed this at a generous decibel level, and interjected a chant in a soft, hushed voice. "Fu jingle mingle tingle. Fu jingle mingle tingle." His vocal volume returned. "I'm an American citizen. I was in the Marines! I have the right to pursue happiness! Make me happy --let me out of here!"

Lance Corporal Walters addressed him cautiously. Even though the Guardsman held a rifle, he sensed this new detainee could offer a large serving of whoop-ass. "Sir, there are people waiting ahead of you. You'll be able to speak to someone in charge as soon as they get to you."

"Nobody strips me down to my birthday suit. Your damned metal detector's broke! Ever hear of preventive maintenance? They ever inspect that machine?" He took a deep breath and murmured "Fu jingle mingle tingle." Seeing the Lance Corporal's discomfort, he added, "I served in 'Nam; a head wound left my gears a little out of sync, if you know what I mean. The mantra helps me get hold of myself."

While Walters conjured an appropriate response, the East Indian businesswoman pounded on the snack machine, jeopardizing her perfect nails. Unsuccessful, she strode purposefully in Walters' direction. "Sergeant…"

"I'm a Lance Corporal, Ma'am," explained Walters.

She ignored the distinction. "You can't expect us to live on what's in those machines. Some of us have been here for hours. How long is this going to take?"

"Ma'am, I don't determine that. My job is to maintain order in this Holding Area. Up to other personnel to decide when to release you."

"Will they take dinner orders?"

"I don't believe so; no, Ma'am."

"How am I supposed to get through this without chocolate?"

From across the room, the big ex-Marine's voice boomed, "Why do they want to inspect my junk?"

Both questions seemed equally sensible and as meaningful as anything else that day.

Chapter 3

DETENTION REPORT, 05 June 201X

FROM: Logan International Airport TSA
TO: TSA Administrator
CC: Department of Homeland Security
RE: Holding Area; Detainees as of 1830 hours
This Detention Report is submitted in accordance with Homeland Security Directive 4772 and with TSA Administrative Rule AXIHS 725.3b.

The following persons were detained by TSA at the Logan International Airport Holding Facility between 0730 and 1830 this date.

PRIORITY DETAINEES:

Emery Palmer, 44, US citizen. Detained at 0915. Identification (which includes an employee badge and appears to be in order) says Palmer is a Methodist minister serving as prison chaplain at the Federal Correctional Institute of Sheridan, Oregon. He claims to be returning from the European Association of Biblical Studies Conference in Vienna. Facial recognition software identifies him as Mahmoud Sabad, one of the terrorists who poisoned the Milan water supply last month. If his identity is confirmed as Sabad, he'll be turned over to Interpol. Currently held for questioning.

Ted McGregor, 29, US citizen. Detained at 1125. Name on passport illegible due to coffee stain. Appears he tried to obscure his identity. His cell contains the phone number of known associate of a 9/11 terrorist. Claims to be Colorado auto mechanic returning from a technical training course in Boston. Cell phone confiscated and subject held for questioning.

Vivi Huarochiri, 16, naturalized citizen. Detained at 1340. Daughter of Peruvian father, Chilean mother. Her uncle is Peru's ambassador to Finland. Father retained Peruvian citizenship; mother is naturalized U. S. citizen. Subject's been in US since she was two. Parents own a 5-star restaurant in Dallas. She flew from Dallas to Orlando, to Boston. Refuses to state purpose of travel. Her IP address appears in records of several hackers currently under investigation. Possible connection to WikiLeaks. On our Watch List. Held for questioning.

ALSO DETAINED:

Glenda Tramboy, 52, US citizen. Detained at 1235. Former history instructor at St. Louis Community College in Missouri. Divorced, no children. Laid off last year; currently unemployed. Passport indicates she was in Cyprus the week of the Nicosia attack and in Egypt during the Mosque Massacre. Subject being held until we can verify the coincidence is non-meaningful.

Navya Ghazal, 46, naturalized citizen. Detained at 1357. Born in Mumbai, India. Currently Southwestern Division VP of Boldwell Cankor commercial real estate in San Diego. She was returning from a business trip. Married to a physician, Dr. Mitra Ghazal. Second cousin Sai Ghazal is known member of terrorist organization Jama'atul Mujahideen Bangladesh. Subject claims to never have met or known her cousin. Held for questioning.

Raven Ferrera, 33, US citizen. Detained at 1615. Ferrera, a TV reporter, entered airport security with a weapon concealed on her person and plastic explosives (without detonator) concealed in a carry-on. Claims she is on assignment to expose vulnerabilities in airport security, and that her station cleared the exercise with TSA headquarters. Detained awaiting confirmation. If exercise cannot be confirmed, Ferrera will be arrested. If it is confirmed, strongly suggest POTUS be notified ASAP, as it will be televised nationally within 24 hours and could have political ramifications.

DeVille Tiamante, 67, US citizen. Detained at 1710. Ex-U.S. Marine. Sustained service-related head injury during Vietnam War. Mother from Detroit; father an American Samoan. Currently resides in New Orleans. Set off alarm when walking through the metal detector. Pat-down revealed nothing. Removed belt, wallet, jewelry, etc. Found no reasons for alarm signal. When asked to disrobe completely in presence of male security guard, detainee became verbally hostile. Held pending further instructions.

The civil service typist who prepared the Detention Report turned to her coworker. "Wanna bet which one of these sets the Administrator's hair on fire?"

"He's probably already dialing 1600 Pennsylvania Avenue."

Chapter 4

President Peabody's Chief of Staff, Roger Shellish, ran through the day's schedule. "At 1:30 PM, you meet with Manny Jimenez, leader of the Congressional Hispanic Caucus. He hopes for a remedy to that situation in San Antonio."

Peabody nodded. He walked to his desk and began skimming the top briefing folder. "What else?"

"The ambassador from China who's not really an ambassador from China has requested a non-meeting." Roger made a weird attempt to wink. "So I didn't schedule it for 4:15 PM."

Peabody looked at his Chief of Staff. "That's the best Alice-in-Wonderland-speak I've heard since Obama justified the drone program."

"Um, well, sir, as I'm sure you're aware, technically the officially recognized Chinese government is the People's Republic of China in Beijing. An ambassador appointed by the Chinese leaders in Taiwan, who were ousted in the Communist revolution, isn't in some senses a Chinese ambassador you want to be meeting with officially."

"Is he or isn't he an ambassador from China?" Peabody pressed him, pretending to be irked.

"Sir, the Republic of China government doesn't really hold sovereignty over the island of Taiwan. Not legally, not officially. You know about the Treaty of 1974?"

"Of course. I even know the place was once called Formosa." Peabody's eyes twinkled as Roger realized he was being played.

"The press's copy of your schedule says at 4:15 PM you're taking an hour off for personal reasons."

"Thank you, Roger." Peabody quickly processed the implications. "This ambassador risked coming here despite the diplomatic sensitivities?" His eyebrows rose with the question. "Guess I'd better brush up on Sun Tzu's Art of War."

Roger smiled ruefully. "Couldn't hurt, sir."

Peabody had just returned from reassuring the inventors of Bird's Nest Soup when Roger appeared at his elbow. The Chief of Staff informed the President, *sotto voce*, "TSA Administrator Bertholt needs to speak to you right away." He handed him a cell phone.

Peabody nodded. The Office of the Presidency required an exquisite blend of chess moves and manure manufacture, but wondering 'What next?' was rarely an issue.

The President skimmed the Detention Report on the laptop Roger provided, then spoke into the phone. "Bud, I assume you've already ordered clown suits for this team of yours in Boston." He barely listened to his TSA Administrator's response. "Exactly what does it mean that a subject is being held 'until a coincidence can be verified as non-meaningful'? Just how the hell does one do that?" He paused to let the sting be fully felt. "You tolerated it when your team in Miami failed every audit for a year. You hired that nephew of yours to run the Boston team, and if this is an example of business as usual at Logan, I'm not impressed. You tolerate incompetence, Bud, but I don't. Tomorrow you'll submit your resignation." He terminated the call while the Administrator was still sputtering excuses.

The Chief of Staff said, "Sorry to have interrupted you, sir. He said it was a matter of extreme importance. I thought perhaps a hijacking."

"That man wouldn't know a crisis if it ran up his leg and bit his johnson. I wonder if they called it a johnson before ole Lyndon," Peabody mused. "The TSA polls lower than syphilis. This Boston incident is two days of media coverage at most." Peabody handed the laptop and cell phone back to Roger. "Frankly, I think we should contract our airport security out to the Israelis. They don't torment 98-year-olds in wheelchairs. But I've been told it wouldn't be politic."

"With all due respect, sir, the Israelis don't have the same understanding of civil rights as we do."

"You must be referring to the pre-Patriot Act Era."

Roger Shellish looked at Peabody, remembering days when the Chief Executive's brow was less furrowed. "Getting back to what's politic…"

"Yes?"

"Press Secretary Fondew requests a meeting with you tomorrow morning to formulate a response to Nate Festring."

Peabody consulted his e-calendar. "Give her the 9:15 slot. What's Festring done now?"

"He issued a new tirade against your tax reform proposal today."

"Damn! Thought I might have him with me on this. Did he at least support eliminating the alternative minimum tax?"

"I'm not really sure, sir. He was, um, rude and non-factual." Peabody gave him an inquiring look. Roger continued, "He suggested you must be having a secret affair with a woman who's persuading you to adopt liberal tax policies."

Peabody let that sink in. "A secret affair, eh? Well, Festring would lose his radio audience if he started feeding them facts. They need a steady diet of Pablum and prevarication."

As afternoon sun light-footed across the Oval Office rug, Peabody reviewed the mound of paperwork on his desk. He welcomed the interruption when his private line rang with a call from Dr. Henigson, his daughter Sarantha's therapist.

"Mr. President, I'm sorry, but Sarantha's cutting again."

"Cutting classes?"

"No, sir. Cutting herself. Again."

Peabody let out a long, slow breath. "Same recommendations as before?"

"Yes, Mr. President."

Somehow this put Festring's blather in proportion. Peabody buzzed for his Chief of Staff. "Let's wrap this day, shall we? Oh, and Roger?"

"I'll have Bertholt's resignation statement ready tomorrow."

"Careful, or I'll start calling you Radar." President Basho Samuels Peabody headed for the private second-floor dining room. As he traveled the windowed corridors, he paused to watch angry protesters picketing along Pennsylvania Avenue --ordinary citizens who could sense democracy yielding to plutocracy but didn't have the vocabulary to describe it. A fractal of civic disenchantment, their numbers increased every day. That fractal continually unfolded, replicated and multiplied as did the frustrations most Americans felt about their government. Demonstrations had gotten out of control in Milwaukee and Phoenix. What was the death toll now – three, four protestors and a National Guardsman?

The country had been primed for violence by the incompetence and overreach of government agencies like the TSA, and the uncompromising greed, hatred and ignorance of a percentage of its citizens. Should I call an impromptu meeting with them, Peabody wondered; try to ease their fears and answer their questions? He thought about what could and couldn't be changed in government, and the constraints that prevented even the most reasonable improvements. The citizens raising high their protest signs probably didn't know or much care that the filibuster wasn't an ideal tool for a bicameral non-parliamentarian government. Festring, cable TV, bloggers and Tweeters had convinced them that governing principles were either black

37

or white. They didn't know or much care that good governing principles fell into nuanced gray areas.

He fingered the brass Bobbie whistle in his slacks pocket. More accurately, he fingered what he told people was a Bobbie whistle. Only he and Demetra Phillips, the ex-fiancée who gave it to him, knew it was actually a Max Factor lipstick case designed to look like a Bobbie whistle. It served as the perfect worry stone for the President. He turned away from the protesters and continued toward the dining room.

His daughter hadn't yet arrived. Good. Peabody took the opportunity to tell Marcel, the Kitchen Supervisor, that when Sarantha dined tonight, every knife was to be accounted for. His daughter did enough damage with razors, nail files, and scissors; he wasn't going to let her abscond with a carving knife.

Peabody sipped a Sea Smoke pinot noir until Sarantha entered and grazed his cheek with a kiss. "Hey, Dad."

"Sarantha. How was your day?"

She abandoned any pretense of genuine interaction with her father. "What are we having?"

"Lamb chops, honey." As soon as the words left his mouth, he recalled her attitude toward eating cuddly baby animals. Uh, oh. "With spinach and baby potatoes."

Sarantha seemed to morph into a hissing feline action hero. She stood and screamed, "I will *not* eat this! I don't know how you can slaughter those innocent…"

The dinner was served.

"Sit down. Marcel, please have the kitchen prepare an alternative." Marcel zipped into the kitchen to command a grilled cheese, tomato, and basil on sourdough, Sarantha's standard. Peabody downed more wine and observed the long sleeves his daughter wore this warm June evening. When the grilled cheese was served, Sarantha ate like he'd been starving her.

"Did you know there's a band called Grilled Cheese?" Peabody asked. "Maybe you'd enjoy their ..." It was a feeble attempt at rapport and he knew it, but what the hell were they supposed to talk about?

Sarantha rolled her eyes at him. "This is the only kind of grilled cheese I like."

The therapist told him his daughter cut herself because the pain of the cuts somehow made her feel more alive, less numb. Where in such a strange and vicious cycle could a father jump in to break it? The most powerful executive in the world summoned his courage. "Dr. Henigson called me today. She says you've been skipping your appointments." He paused a moment. "And...and she told me about the cutting." His nod indicated her sleeves. "Has anything changed for you? Someone bothering you at school? Or..."

"Dad, drop it!"

Peabody took in his daughter's thick blond hair pulled back in a minimalist braid; her pouty, pierced lips, and tense shoulders. The pure gray eyes she inherited from her mother and the hint of his Native American cheekbones lent her a classic beauty. Her face sprouted several acne blemishes that probably seemed hideous to her.

"Just keep your appointments with Dr. Henigson. If you don't, we'll need to…"

"All right! All right! Gawd!" She pushed her plate away and sulked.

Well, Peabody thought, perhaps I'll have the Secret Service pick up Nate Festring and lock him in a room with Sarantha for a few days. His money would be on Sarantha.

Chapter 5

Afternoon faded into evening in the Logan International Airport Security Holding Room. At intervals someone would be summoned for interrogation. No matter how many logical explanations, verifiable identifications, or requests for an attorney were proffered, Boston TSA had not released a single detainee.

Lance Corporal Walters felt perplexed. People ordinarily were detained an hour, maybe two. If they were found to be actual threats, they were taken into custody by Homeland Security. But today was different. He was about to rotate out of his shift and some of the folks detained this morning were still here. What was going on?

In an office rife with LeRoy Neiman reproductions and Aeron chairs, Andrea Tarmini, the airport's liaison to TSA, broke out in a sweat despite the air conditioning. "Rudy," she said to the current TSA Manager for the Boston region, "you've still got seven people in the holding room. Some of them have been there more than ten hours."

"Read this!" Rudy folded a letter into a paper airplane and launched it across his desk.

Tarmini caught and read it. "Holy shit! Your uncle fired you? I thought he pulled strings to get you this job?"

"Apparently his balls have been shaved by President Peabody himself. He's being forced to resign tomorrow, something about a lapse in procedures. This much I know – some of the people in Holding are responsible. So I figure, why not share my pain with the assholes who caused all this?"

"It's probably the scam by that TV reporter. She said it had been cleared by headquarters. Didn't your uncle warn you they were coming?"

He shrugged. "I don't concern myself with the details of day to day operations. I'm more of a big picture kinda guy. And I'm…" He paused and clicked his laptop mouse a few times, then continued, "…1,319 emails behind in my Inbox." Tarmini gasped. He looked at her. "Who's got time? Anyway, letting some of these people stew for a while will make them think twice before they jack around with the TSA again. What's the worst they can do to me? I'm fired anyway, right?" Rudy lit a cigar and sent smoke rings toward the ceiling.

"I see you're in 'let them eat cake' mode."

"Huh?"

"Never mind. Be careful, Rudy; the smoke alarms still work even if you don't."

"Fuck 'em; fuck 'em all."

"Detain U.S. citizens long enough and some of them are going to sue you."

"With my credit card debt, after a few months of unemployment, I won't even be suit-worthy. Shit, how am I going to find another job in this economy?"

42

"I don't know, Rudy. Got any more uncles?"

When Andrea Tarmini returned to the Holding
Facility, her business suit was wrinkled and her eyes had
more bags than the luggage conveyers. She wasn't used to
working at 10:45 PM. She asked Vivi Huarochiri to
accompany her. The teen had been called in for questioning
twice already. The first time she'd returned with a defiant
look. The second time she was more subdued; things clearly
had not gone the way the girl had anticipated. Now
summoned for a third time, every cliché about Latin
temperament emerged. Vivi fled to the far side of the room
and screeched about abuse in English, Spanish and
Spanglish. When Tarmini tried to physically drag her from
the Holding Facility, Vivi fought like a honey badger on
meth.

Deville placed a hand the size of a hubcap on
Tarmini's shoulder. "I'm DeVille Tiamante. Why are you
messing with this girl? What's she done?"

"DeVille? What kind of name is that?" Tarmini
allowed her curiosity to distract her from the task at hand.

"DeVille was the finest, shiniest name that my
mother, Lagonda Bugatti Jones, could come up with."

Vivi took advantage of the interlude to stomp on
Tarmini's instep. A moaning Tarmini assigned the task to
Lance Corporal Walters' replacement, who successfully
dragged Vivi from the Holding Facility to parts unknown.

A mutual awareness of 'there but for the grace of
God go I' began to bond the remaining detainees. They
rearranged their chairs so they could hear one another

43

without being overheard by Big Brother. As the hours passed, they called loved ones and told them not to worry, and hoped that wasn't false comfort. They leaned in close to listen, and shared the reasons they had been detained. Half jesting, half serious, they commiserated with and vented to one another. Slowly the conversation drifted to families, summer Little League, Golden doodles, titanium versus ceramic joint replacements, whatever happened to that actor from The Wire, and the best strategy for Texas Hold 'Em.

By now any expectation of catching their flights, returning home to loved ones tonight, or consulting an attorney had come and gone. Something was clearly amiss. Navya was certain there'd been another terrorist attack; Ted suspected an airline crash even though they hadn't seen anything on TV. Whatever had occurred, the feeling among the detainees was that they were no one's priority, at least not tonight.

Vivi was escorted back to the Holding Area, apparently having held up well. "I told those *culeros* nothing! Nothing! Only that I demand to talk to my attorney. *Mi tio* knows people who will create plenty of shit for them if they keep harassing me. They don't like it, *andate a la mierda!*"

"Vivi, are the things they say true about you? Are you really a Wiki Leaks hacker?" Glenda wanted to know.

"Could I hack into a system? In my sleep. Am I a terrorist? No. I told those *pendejos* this already. What really pisses me off is that they won't let me see a lawyer. Isn't that supposed to be one of our rights?"

"Big government doesn't respect our rights," Ted declared. "I mean, how dangerous could Vivi be?" He hesitated, making an internal decision. "I haven't been totally honest with you about why I'm here. They did detain me for the coffee stain on my passport. But what I didn't tell you is that when they questioned me the second time, it was about a number on my cell phone. My brother Andy's number. He lives in San Diego and was assigned a number that used to belong to one of the 9/11 terrorists. When the terrorist died, the phone company re-assigned the number to my brother." A few heads turned. "It's not my brother's fault, is it, that his phone company did that? Anyway, they're checking my story. Once they do that, they should cut me loose."

Glenda's wild eyebrows seemed to swerve as she shook her head in sympathy. "I don't think the TSA folks here are the brightest."

"Well, stupidity in government is hardly a novel concept," Navya chimed in. "A while ago I read that the feds spent nearly half a million of our tax dollars to explore the relationship between gender and glaciers! What next? A study on whether innie belly button people and outie belly button people relate to trees the same way?"

"And remember those famous $700 toilet seats and $200 hammers for the military? Or was it $200 toilet seats and $700 hammers?" Raven joined in.

"My favorite," said Ted, "was when NASA spent a million in tax dollars to develop a ballpoint pen that would let the ink flow without gravity, so it could write in space." He paused to deliver his punch line, "The Russians decided to use pencils; cost maybe a dime each."

"Journalists and reporters like me can spotlight that kind of waste," said Raven, "but it continues anyway. Even with sequestration, we still spend tax dollars on nonsense."

Navya glanced at her Rolex. "Damn, I missed that special of The Voice!"

Emery Palmer spoke for the first time since introducing himself as a Methodist minister.. "I've heard that people really like that show, but I've never watched it. What makes it so special?"

"¿De done eres?" from Vivi.

Navya explained to Emery, "It's like a singing contest on TV. The audience votes for their favorites."

"And the votes actually matter. Eventually, one singer beats out all the competition and gets a music contract," Glenda piped in. "I wish our political votes were that effective. I mean, we call ourselves a democracy, but how many times do we vote for a sensible energy policy, fairer taxes, or against going into some crazy war – and nothing happens?"

"I'm about to make something happen in the energy field," Raven enthused. "Serious! I'm so psyched. When I return to L.A., my station manager promised to let me move ahead with my new TV show, Power Up! It'll do for renewable energy what American Idol and The Voice did for singing. Contestants will come on the show; demonstrate their clean energy inventions, and viewers will vote each week for the best one."

"Now that's a sharp idea. Democratic and entrepreneurial." Navya paused thoughtfully. "Sometimes I think ordinary people like us—especially business people who are used to solving problems –could handle almost any problem better than the government can."

Glenda's cell phone rang; she moved away from the group to take the call. She returned shortly. "My mother just passed away. I missed my chance to say good-bye!" Her eyes brimmed with tears. The group huddled around her and offered sympathetic murmurs and hugs. Her grief was tinged with anger. "It's one thing for Congress to bungee jump over fiscal cliffs, or for Super Pacs and lobbyists to pull the puppet strings. But government doesn't just affect wallets; it affects our hearts, our relationships, our lives! If an incompetent federal agency can keep me from saying good-by to my dying mother…" She paced around, occasionally kicking an innocent chair leg for release. "I don't know the answer, but I know we can do better!"

"People say they could do better than politicians," Ted said slowly, "but, hell, I'm a mechanic. I don't know the first thing about writing legislation. It's probably a lot harder than we think." He scanned the Holding Area, counting heads. "Really, what could seven ordinary citizens do?"

"If those 'ordinary citizens' were named Washington, Adams, Jefferson, Franklin, Hancock, Monroe, and Madison," Glenda said, "one hell of a lot! We could start a revolution!"

Chapter 6

Tongues loosened and politics again became the prime topic. They talked about how economic crises, terrorist attacks, school shootings, grinding wars, and an ineffective public school system had altered the American spirit most of them had grown up with into something unrecognizable. Glenda wondered if government 'of the people, by the people, and for the people' may, indeed, have perished from this earth with the Citizens United decision. The conversation distracted her from her grief. She pulled from her history instructor days, contributing factoids about Ben Franklin's Francophilia, James Monroe's hemorrhoids, and Thomas Jefferson's dalliances.

Maybe it was because they were gathered only a few miles from where Paul Revere saddled up. Or maybe it was because, as Glenda had reminded them, that if a handful of people could form a new nation, then it wasn't entirely unbelievable that a handful of citizens could change the dirty diapers of democracy. Whatever the reason, Don't Tread on Me magic was in the air.

Raven exuberantly exclaimed, "All right! Let's figure out our agenda!"

Ted responded. "Let's clean up all the red tape that costs us tons of money! That would help our debt. Government just can't keep borrowing money from China. Money's a finite resource. Liberals don't seem to get that."

Emery turned to Ted. "Money is a finite resource. So why do we spend so much of our treasure fighting unnecessary wars?"

DeVille stood up from the table and moved into Emery's personal space. He even rocked back on his heels a bit. "You some kind of pacifist?"

"Yes, I am a pacifist," Emery replied as he, too, stood up. He was six inches shorter than DeVille. "I'm a prison chaplain. I spend my life looking at the fruits of violence."

Lance Corporal Walters cleared his throat and motioned for the big man to move away. DeVille took a step back, looking at the clergyman thoughtfully. "Fu jingle mingle tingle. You're a prison chaplain. I'm an ex-Marine. We're gonna see things different."

Emery remained standing, looking DeVille in the eye. The big man recognized the courage this took and sat back down.

"Getting back to your point," Emery said to Ted, "Don't you think that our exaggerated military spending causes America's budget woes?"

"Well, I guess we know the liberal in our group," Ted said lightly, glancing at the others.

"Emery's not the only liberal here. I've voted Democrat in every election," said Raven. "And by the way, don't assume every Democrat is anti-military. My fiancé is an Army Public Affairs Officer assigned to NATO."

And so it went. One by one, each person's political stripes were revealed. Among these seven ordinary airport travelers were two Democrats, one Republican, one Tea Party member, one Independent, and two who had never voted and didn't want to start-- a coincidental mirror of where the country was when it wasn't in line at Starbuck's.

"Maybe the budget priorities aren't the best issue for us to start with," Navya tactfully intervened. "Tell us more about this Power Up! show. Will it cover all kinds of energy, or just renewable energy?"

Raven's face glowed with passion for her new project. "Clean, renewable energy. That's where we need to look for big breakthroughs, big solutions."

"And why is that?" asked Ted. "Are you one of those who believe car exhaust is melting the polar ice caps?"

Raven let fly. "You Tea Partyers are in such denial! Yes, I believe in climate change. We need to stop putting this country's resources into fossil fuel shit, and invest in renewables!"

Emery looked uncomfortable at the four-letter word.

"Civility, lady!" DeVille towered over them again. The tone of his voice modeled the civility he requested. "Let's keep it clean."

"Yes, that's what I want to do—keep the earth clean!" Raven's humor drew a chuckle from some, frowns from others.

"You're a socialist; you want to destroy American capitalism," replied an unamused Ted. "Hard working people who drill for oil or mine coal are out of jobs; parts of this country are going down the tubes, because of dreamers who believe America can run on rainbows and wishful thinking!"

"That's not fair, Ted," objected Raven as a palpable tension filled the room. "I'm not against jobs. Just against jobs that pollute the planet. Green energy holds such potential; I mean, once we find a method of renewable energy generation that's economical, it'll give US capitalism the biggest boost ever!"

"A lot you care about capitalism! That's such bullshi…"

DeVille placed a hand on Ted's shoulder. "No need for those kinds of words. No need. You can say bull crap. Bull turds. Bullwinkle..."

"Who made you Hall Monitor?" Ted asked. Turning back to Raven, he continued. "I don't believe for a minute that you care about a strong economy. All you want is socialism."

Perhaps someone should have reminded the budding revolutionaries that they were detained against their will, removed from the normal Fruit Loop of everyday life, and they had low blood sugar. Tempers flared. There was a palpable fissure in their united revolutionary vision.

DeVille clapped his humungous hands together and quieted the group. Further discussion was negated when the guard's radio crackled. The soldier listened, glanced at the clock, and conveyed the news. "To recover your belongings and leave the airport legally, you'll need releases from the TSA office. They open again at oh-eight-hundred tomorrow. Until then, you're not permitted to leave the airport premises. I have to equip each of you with an ankle monitor before I can let you out of here. I've been authorized to bring in cots, blankets and pillows. When each of you has your ankle monitor, this door will remain unlocked and you can come and go throughout the airport."

Chapter 7

They weren't thrilled about having to stay until morning, but every one of them accepted the ankle monitor in order to leave the Holding Facility. From a terminal corridor, Navya exclaimed, "It's 2:20 AM! I'm famished! Are any airport restaurants still open?"

They explored the terminal and found only one open facility, a bar, with one person, a bartender, holding down the fort. While well stocked with liquor, the bar's food offerings were restricted to maraschino cherries, olives and cocktail onions. There was a modest kitchen in back, but it had closed at midnight. After explaining how long they had been detained and that he was a chef, DeVille asked the bartender if he could use the kitchen. The bartender unlocked the kitchen, but added, "I can't let you into the freezer or pantry areas. I don't have the keys." DeVille started to say something, then decided not to.

"My stomach's rumbling," Ted informed those in the little group who hadn't heard it rumble themselves. He began devouring cocktail onions.

"I feel queasy, lightheaded," said Emery, "like when I fast for Lent."

"Get yourselves a drink," suggested DeVille. "We'll be back with food soon." He grabbed Vivi by her elbow and began a jog down the terminal corridor, stopping by various food joints. Vivi was in awe of how quickly DeVille could pick locks to access the little eateries. They loaded foods into paper bags: onions, vinegar, spices, meats, fish, tomatoes, pickles, potatoes, peppers, clam chowder, even chop suey from a Chinese fast food joint.

On the way back to the bar, DeVille turned to Vivi. "You some kinda hacker, right?"

"I know my way around computers. *¿Por qué?*"

DeVille's gaze rose to the security cameras in the terminal hallway. "Can you take us off those surveillance cameras?

Vivi shrugged, apparently glad it was, by her standards, a minor request. "Can't do nothing till they give me my laptop again, but once I have it, *no problemo*. I'll snuff the GPS tracking for our ankle monitors, too—*pinche chingaderas* --otherwise they'll know where we went."

When they returned to the bar, the stranded travelers had assembled smaller tables into one large communal table. DeVille began preparing the food in the kitchen and told Vivi to go get dinner orders.

"I'm not a waitress; you go get dinner orders."

DeVille crooked his head at an angle and said, "I'm not asking for water from the moon, cher. Now go."

For some reason, Vivi yielded. Given no restrictions, each person ordered whatever he or she wanted --- pot roast, enchiladas, masala dosa, cheeseburger, and of course, Boston clam chowder. No one actually expected to get what they ordered. But DeVille worked culinary magic. Within 45 minutes, everyone had an appealing meal in front of them. Maybe not exactly what was ordered, but something close to it that tasted great. Emery Palmer offered a five-second grace. By the time DeVille brought out his own dinner, the food had given folks a second wind.

"How'd you do this, DeVille? You're amazing!" exclaimed Raven.

"I cook. At the Pourquoi Pas restaurant in New Orleans. That's what I do. I like to make folks happy."

"And you do it so well! This chicken tastes heavenly. Do you own the restaurant, DeVille?" Navya's nerves soothed as she dipped her twelfth bite of chicken breast into its savory sauce.

"Part owner. Bought into it so they'd let me cook. Get to wear the chef's hat, too!" The facial expressions of several in the group reflected a certain unease. He continued, "I'm a little bit off, yes, I know. But I have a good life. I have happiness."

They felt less angry and more thoughtful now--a snicker from the Universe because more blood now flowed to stomachs than to brains. Vivi returned to shark-infested conversational waters. "You know, back there...when we argued, we sounded as bad as the assholes in Congress." It was a stinging condemnation and they flinched at its truth.

"Are we sure we're not as bad as the, er, characters in Congress?" asked Emery. "Politicians don't come into this world to be jerks. But we vote them into positions where temptation constantly lures them."

"Come on, Emery," this from Glenda. "Those bastards sell democracy to the highest bidder! Why do you think we're having so many problems with the government?"

"If there's one thing I've learned as a minister and prison counselor, it's that each of us is self-centered in some way; everyone experiences greed or pride or hatred. 'For all have sinned and come short of the glory...'"

"Yeah, yeah; spare me the Bible quotes if you want me to hold my dinner down," said Glenda.

Changing the subject, Navya gestured down the corridor toward the Holding Area, "Back there, I felt like we were on the cusp of something important. But here we sit, aware we have other lives in other places that in no way connect all of us. It's hard to believe we could somehow align ourselves well enough to change the course of government. Just saying it sounds rather arrogant, maybe even stupid."

"We'd probably have trouble figuring out where to sit in a taxi if we shared one, let alone how to reform the government," snapped Raven.

DeVille stood, looked around and waited until he had everyone's attention. "We enjoyed our late meal. Ted, you had a cheeseburger, right?"

Ted nodded. DeVille looked at Raven. "And you, cher? Clam chowder, right?"

"It was delicious."

DeVille turned to Ted. "Do you think Raven wanted a good meal?"

"Well, sure."

"But according to you, she should've ordered a cheeseburger if she wanted a good meal. Right?"

"She's got her own taste buds. Personally I can't stand clam chowder. But that doesn't mean she didn't want a good meal."

"So someone can want the same thing as you – you both wanted a good meal – yet you go about it in different ways?" DeVille was on a roll.

"Well, yes…"

"Then maybe don't say Raven doesn't want a good economy just because she wants clean energy." DeVille turned to Raven. "And don't say Ted wants to pollute the planet if he wants good jobs for people. It's not so hard, cher. Cut each other a bit of slack. Be happy!"

Ted said, "I'll drink to that," and swallowed the last of his Sam Adams.

"Let's toss it around one more time; see if we want to give it a try." Glenda suggested as one eyebrow jumped the C train. "If we're really going to try to pull off even a minor 'revolution,' we need to organize. To get things done, we'll need resources."

Raven spoke up. "I'm a TV reporter; I have media contacts. And I live in L.A., which means I know actors. Might be helpful."

"I can hack into nearly any computer system," admitted Vivi. "And since we'll need some way to connect with one another, I'll create a secure chat room so we can all meet online." She whipped out her cell phone. "I need your email addresses and phone numbers to tell you where to find the chat room when it's ready. Do not try to contact me first." She tossed her now-loose dark curls nervously. "I have ways to keep *todo seguro*, but I'll need some time." As the discussion progressed, people entered their contact info into Vivi's phone.

"I can cook," began DeVille. "We all gotta eat. And I know how to handle weapons."

"So we've got media contacts, actors, computer wizardry, cooking, and gun skills. Not bad," Glenda summarized. "What else?"

Emery frowned. "Frankly it makes me nervous when you mention weapons. What kind of tactics do we intend to use for this "revolution?"

"Exposing politicians who lie?"

"Social media campaigns?"

"I can plant viruses…"

"Maybe we do it all through Raven's TV show?"

DeVille managed to keep all the jingles and tingles to a minimum. "We want the American people to be happy, right? Let's make them laugh! Make them see how silly it is for a great country like ours to be stuck in the mud."

Raven smiled. "I could come up with ideas about how to fool the media. I mean, I'm a reporter, right? I know how little they check out story leads. We might even have some fun ourselves!"

Emery smiled. "Now humor's a tactic I can get behind! Almost everyone responds to it. And as long as we keep this non-violent, I can offer the power of prayer. I'll pray we do the right thing for America."

Glenda rolled her eyes. "Maybe we can also write a letter to Santa Claus or light a candle to Zeus."

DeVille looked directly at Glenda and whispered, "A little respect for the man of the cloth." Few of the others looked particularly impressed with prayer as a strategy but Glenda had been the only one bold enough to mock.

Instead of pleading his case in theological terms, Emery simply said, "My brother went to Georgetown Law School; he was friends with the President's Chief of Staff. That might help."

"That could definitely help!" This from Glenda. "I think we'll need something like a modern version of *Common Sense*. I could probably create that."

"What's *Common Sense*?" asked Vivi.

"A pamphlet written by Thomas Paine that sparked the American Revolution. Nowadays it would probably be a blog. It was written in plain language so everyone could understand it. It talked about democracy and principles of good government."

"Good government. Don't hear those two words together often." Ted commented.

"I remember a talent DeVille forgot to tell you about," said Vivi, interrupting the impending digression, "He can pick locks!"

DeVille squirmed and began a fu jingle mingle tingle series.

Raven asked, "How about you, Ted?"

59

"I'm a damned good auto mechanic. And I started taking private pilot lessons a few months ago. Don't have my license yet. Not sure how any of that can help, but…" He shrugged his shoulders.

Glenda reassured him. "No problem. I'm sure you'll find ways to contribute. She continued, "We're going to need funds. The first American Revolution had John Hancock, the richest man in New England, picking up the tab. Washington and Jefferson weren't paupers either, and they helped out. I've been out of work for a while; I can't provide the deep pockets."

"I can," offered Navya. "My family is well off; I have considerable funds at my disposal. If we really try to accomplish something positive for this country, I'll fund it."

They discussed their nascent mini-revolution for another half hour. Glenda looked down at her notes. "So we'll work together as a team of individuals, and not on behalf of any political party. Everyone on board?" Everyone consented. She continued, "Since we live in different places, we'll do most of our communication online. Vivi will let us know the best way to stay under the radar. We good with that?"

Ted said to Glenda, "You're kind of our leader already. Let's vote and make it official!" He turned to everyone. "Raise your hand if you want Glenda as our, uh, coordinator, our, uh…"

Navya tossed out a suggestion from her world of business, "Our primary contact?"

"Right," agreed Ted. Everyone lifted a hand except Glenda, who smiled.

"Thank you for that honor. I'll try to do Thomas Paine proud. I do have a suggestion before we get rolling on this. If we are going to find ways to move beyond the usual stalemate positions, it would be good if everyone stated one thing they feel so passionate about that they don't ever want to compromise on that topic. For example, my pet peeve is how watered down our democracy has become. I mean, as a country, we vote once every four years, if that. But the rest of the time, monumental decisions are made for us by people, agencies, and courts that we have no say in. Like the TSA preventing me from seeing my dying mother. What kind of democracy is that?" She tugged unconsciously at one of her earrings, doing an inadvertent Carol Burnett imitation. "The thing I won't give up is empowered democracy-- turning the country back over to its citizens."

"I'm for Open Source everything!" declared Vivi. She turned to Glenda. "That's major empowered democracy; you should be able to roll with that."

"I don't know what this means, cher, this 'open source everything,'" DeVille admitted.

"It's a step toward Open Government, Open Society," Vivi explained. "It starts with the free sharing of information, like software codes, free university courses online, or military intelligence; stuff like that. Instead of some jackoff politician making decisions, you give the people the information and let them make their own decisions. You 'Open Source' it; you let everyone share the information and come up with solutions to problems."

"Doesn't sound very practical to me," Navya said. "Nor very capitalist."

61

"Open Source isn't popular in Hollywood," Raven interjected. "Proprietary law undergirds copyrights and patents. We already lose tons of movie and music money to cyber-theft."

Glenda knew they needed Vivi onboard for her computer skills. She turned to the feisty young woman. "I believe the world is moving toward Open Source everything. We'll get there eventually, but that day will be far in the future. Would it work for you if we took a step in the direction of Open Source everything? How about if we try, like Snowden, to get rid of the NSA's spying on citizens program?" Glenda knew as soon as she'd dropped the name Snowden, she had Vivi.

Vivi thought for all of two seconds. "*Bueno*, I can live with that. The rest of you will probably be dead by the time we live in a fully Open Source world anyway."

The weary travelers puzzled over that, uncertain if she'd just insulted them or agreed with them. The consensus seemed to be that she agreed to narrow her scope a bit, in terms of her no-compromise issue. Like the good community college instructor she was, Glenda again took notes and made a list. She looked around the room. "What about you, Raven?"

"No brainer. Non-polluting sustainable green energy! I want this country to fund research to find several ways to generate green energy and make it so practical that eventually everyone will see the light!"

Glenda noted: Fund new green energy sources – Raven. She looked up. "Ted?"

"The can of worms I'd want to tackle is government red tape – all the ridiculous regulations that screw up the works every time we try to get something done. Read a magazine article that really got my attention. To fix one bridge in New Jersey, a bunch of federal, state and local agencies had to approve the repair. And to get *one* of the many environmental permits required, the builders had to invite Native Americans from all over the country to weigh in on the subject. Some were as far away as Nebraska-- all that just to repair a broken bridge in New Jersey! Oh, and a nurse I was dating told me there are over 140,000 billing categories for Medicare, including 21 for 'spacecraft accidents.' Can you imagine the gnarly mess of regulations and bureaucracy that involved!"

"We need a name for your issue, Ted."

"How about Make Regulation Make Sense?"

"Good one," Glenda commented as she wrote it down. "Navya, what are you vitally passionate about?"

"No one major issue I couldn't compromise on, but I'd like to reserve the right to veto anything that's too detrimental to business. American businesses have a hard enough time competing globally."

Glenda echoed back her request. "OK, Navya will hold veto power over any bill or program we support in order to make sure it's not excessively hard on business."

"I want veto power, too," said Emery. "I'd like to hold veto power for anything that doesn't conform to higher moral values."

"You realize, don't you," Raven asked with LA snark, "that at the very least, we're going to be manipulating the media, planting false stories, and hacking computers?

Exactly how high are these moral standards you want us to abide by?"

"See what you mean," laughed Emery. "What I meant was the 'do no harm' side of moral values. I don't want to be part of anything that's cruel or violent or seriously harmful, in terms of universal moral principles. If one of our ideas moves too close to that boundary, I want veto power."

Glenda once again read from her notes. "Empowered democracy – me. Eliminate NSA's spying on citizens program – Vivi. Veto power to protect business from unreasonable negatives – Navya. Veto power to disapprove something on the grounds that it's immoral – Emery.

Ted turned to DeVille. "That leaves you."

"I want to help people be happy. No compromise! We have the right to life, liberty and the pursuit of happiness!"

Glenda mumbled to herself, "Not exactly sure how we'll manage that one, but you can't argue with happiness." She looked up. "On every other issue, folks, be prepared to compromise. We may have to settle for less than we originally dreamed of, but we'll try to get at least some things done. The things on this list," she raised the note paper, "we'll hold sacred; we won't ask you to compromise on them. But on everything else, be flexible. We do need to do better than Congress."

The inelegant paroxysms of anger and frustration at an incompetent government had dissipated. With full stomachs, yawns began to escape.

Glenda brought up another topic. "You're aware," she warned, "that even if we try to make modest changes to government by manipulating the media or hacking or a caper or two that may not be completely above-board, prosecutors may not appreciate our good intentions. What we're doing will likely be considered civil disobedience. We could be arrested; possibly even go to prison. Are you all OK with that?"

Emery said, "I've been a prison chaplain for many years. Prisons are not kind places. Please, think this through." The darkness of his 5 o'clock shadow seemed a metaphor for his remarks. He addressed the group in a compelling voice and cadence that revealed his pulpit experience. "To create a true political movement, we'd have to trust one another. And let's be honest: I barely know you, and you barely know me. If we're just blowing off steam, fine; nothing wrong with that. We can vent our frustration and forget these conversations ever took place when we're home sleeping in our own beds. But if we're really in this to change our government, we'll inevitably push against people who want to maintain the status quo. And those people could cause us trouble, legal and otherwise."

Ted responded, "I'm in, but only if we don't let our families or friends in on this. I mean, we're the ones taking the risk, not them. I sure don't want to rain trouble down on my mom and dad because of this. I know it'll be a hard promise to keep but…"

Glenda concurred. "Good idea, Ted. If we have to explain time away from our families, we can say we joined a political movement and we're protesting or some such."

DeVille looked at Vivi. "You're young. Get yourself in trouble with the law now and you might lose some choices in life."

Vivi interrupted. *"¡No me importa!* I'm already in trouble for hacking, but I still want to make a difference."

Logan Airport grew mighty quiet in that moment, perhaps as quiet as it had been in Philadelphia the night before the Declaration of Independence was signed. One by one, the stranded travelers looked into each others' faces and began to whisper, "I'm in," "Let's do it," "Yes, for real."

Glenda suggested they head back to the Holding Area to catch some rest before the TSA office opened at eight. Everyone concurred.

DeVille lightened the mood. "In the Marines, we gave our units nicknames—the Thundering Third, Lava Dogs, Hell in a Helmet, stuff like that. Our group should have a name, too."

"Not the Tea Partyers!" declared Raven.

"Not Occupiers!" countered Ted.

A lull in the conversation ensued while everyone brainstormed. Dessert had not been part of their long night's sustenance and Navya was overcome by her sweet tooth. Her hands rummaged through her purse for whatever remaining morsels she could find. Her chocolate-covered cherries were long gone, but throughout their time in the bar and Holding Facility, Navya had retrieved two Hershey kisses and part of a Mars bar from various purse compartments. Now she brought a squished neon yellow marshmallow candy up to her mouth. It left an outline of sugar crystals on her lips. Soon everyone realized what it was.

"I've got it!" Raven exclaimed. "We the Peeps!"

Chapter 8

Dallas, TX: Vivi played with the loose curl hanging near her right eye. She sent a surreptitious glance in the direction of the blond boy who sat near her on the bleachers, the one who smelled like almonds and gym sweat. Flutter, flutter, almond butter. He'd been watching her, too. Vivi noticed the time on her cell -- time for the Peeps to meet. Reluctantly, she stepped down from her high school bleachers, hid in a rest room stall, pulled her iPad from her backpack and booted up. She hoped the older people she'd met at the airport could at least figure out how to log in.

San Diego, CA: Navya sat in her Mercedes in the shaded parking garage of Boldwell Cankor with her car doors locked, savoring gourmet chocolate-covered Bing cherries and trying to woo a particularly desirable yet stubborn client on the phone. She'd explained the property's economic base multiplier to him but he insisted the efficiency percentage wasn't high enough to justify the investment. Navya concocted a story about a rival client itching to get his hands on this investment property. Honesty -- collateral damage in the world of sales-- wasn't always the best narrative. She felt a thrill of excitement when she noticed the time on her car dashboard and told the resistant client she had a call coming in from the other buyer. Meeting time!

Sheridan, OR: Thirteen felonious federal prisoners positioned themselves around the dinner table on the stage of the correctional facility's auditorium, re-enacting the Last Supper. Mean Larry, 326 pounds of muscle, won the role of

Jesus because no one wanted to argue with him about it. Billy, Hassan, and Miguel insisted on royal purple capes. Ed and Diego were garbed in 14th century tunics, the prison theater wardrobe and prop room being limited. Frank demanded the role of St. John and wore a long, flowing thing Emery didn't know the name of... but he rather liked it. Tycho, tats covering his hard body, seemed overly intense about getting into the character of St. Peter. Emery's eyes glanced at the clock above the auditorium stage. "Rehearsal's over, guys. See you Tuesday for Bible study. God bless!"

Los Angeles, CA: Raven was paying her bills online when her cell alarm went off, signaling time for the Peeps connection. The last payment she authorized was to cover $113.49 on her MasterCard from ABUZZ Vibrators. Raven smiled to herself. It had been worth every penny. Next time Will returned home from deployment, she'd share the pleasure with him. MasterCard made her think of Citicard, which made her think of CitiBank, which in turn evoked the name Wachovia. Raven remembered when she could walk into her local bank and not cringe with shame at the things that bank had done. Why do we allow Chase, Bank of America, and others to embarrass us with their corporate behavior? Maybe each of us feels, Raven posited, that we don't have enough leverage. And maybe that's so. Until we bond together, we won't have the advantage of synergy. If we cooperated, but ah, we humans... we humans, not always, but too often, will forego the peace of cooperation for the piece of silver, the piece of real estate, the piece we think we deserve for our striving.

Boulder, CO: Ted picked at the bandage on his finger. He'd sliced it while repairing a radiator at work and the cut was bugging him. He'd had to dodge a lot of questions from his current main squeeze about why he

69

didn't want to accompany her to her bowling tournament, but she finally gave in. He stood in his garage, tinkering with his lawnmower until he heard the buzz of his cell phone alarm. It was time.

St. Louis, MO: While walking Socrates the Havanese, Glenda listened to Chapter 4 of a new audio book, *Grieving the Death of a Parent*. She felt the vibration of her cell phone alarm, and gave Socrates the leash command to head home. Time to further the revolution!

New Orleans, LA: DeVille sprinkled, tasted, and sniffed the entrée he was preparing. Then he sprinkled and tasted and sniffed some more. Vanilla? No. Cinnamon? Maybe. But he didn't want it to taste too… Ah! Cardamom! That was it! A huge smile spread across his face. Yes, cardamom. And maybe the tiniest dash of cayenne. When he glanced at his watch, he ordered a line cook to finish what he'd started. He went into his back office, sat down at the computer and asked the young prep cook to help him get online.

At the online meeting, the Peeps established their agenda. Since Raven's Power Up! TV show had been green-lighted (*green*-lighted, hee hee), they decided to take on her renewable energy project as their first item. There was already a major energy bill in the works in Congress loaded with seed money for more fracking. With luck they may be able to make that work for them.

The goal of clean, green energy seemed least exciting to Ted. In an effort to maintain team cohesion, Glenda suggested that Ted's 'Make Regulation Make Sense' concept be their second goal.

Raven: So what are our next steps?

Glenda: Vivi, do whatever voodoo you need to do to gain access to Congress's copy of the energy bill they're working on. Raven, you have an enormous role in this – use your show to find a powerful, promising green energy source!

Navya: Still not sure how we're going to execute this.

Emery: Sometimes you have to start where you can and, as the Quakers say, 'Way will open.'

Glenda: I'll write a Common Sense-type blog to help distract media and politicos from the energy bill and to stir curiosity about our cause.

By the time their online chat concluded, Glenda thought, "This 'plan' has more holes than Swiss cheese, but it's a start."

DeVille went back to his kitchen and added Swiss cheese to a quiche.

Chapter 9

Raven cruised across the floor with a natural vitality that drew everyone's gaze. She'd been born with what her grandpa called va-va-va-voom. Like Lady Day, she classed up the joint, the joint being an under-budget, cement-floored edifice housing six production studios. Lighting got most of the budget. The studios belonged to a regional network and L.A. affiliate, KCUP-TV, who were grateful for Raven's talent. When she'd approached them with her dream of a competition show for green energy ideas, what could they say? The Voice *con verde*? Why not? They gave her an undesirable Saturday afternoon timeslot, minimal budget and their best wishes. They expected the show to bomb quickly, but if ponying up the money for an initial run of five episodes kept Raven there, it was worth it. And who knew? Maybe the show would become syndicated; isn't that what they all wanted?

"Ready 3, take 3!"

On the set of Power Up!, Raven accepted a glass of wheat grass juice from her production assistant and took a deep breath. They were shooting the fourth episode; previous episodes had thus far resembled Nova meets Rocky & Bullwinkle. During the first show, one contestant fueled a lamp with the luminol in human blood, making their debut rather gory. That contestant competed against a disbarred attorney who swore that Mutt Methane could easily be extracted from the dog poop he'd hauled to the studio in a wheelbarrow. The stink still lingered. The second show stirred protests from animal rights groups when a contestant accidentally killed the 13 jellyfish she used in her bioluminescence project. The third show could've bored a coma victim. The most viable contestant explained in undecipherable jargon how carbon dioxide released in something called 'earth burps' could be captured and converted to electricity, but failed to prove it. Raven saw the handwriting on the KCUP-TV wall. But she was hopeful about today's contestants; staff was getting better at screening them.

"Stand by VDR 1 to cue!"

Nine minutes later Tristan Newberg of Parma, Ohio, a 19-year-old MIT drop-out, explained his green energy project to the show's host. "I got to thinking, what happens when hydraulic fracturing has been used to make fissures in rock… what happens if the state then outlaws fracking? It's happened in a number of places. Seemed like such a waste; I mean, the fractures already exist. I wondered if there was some way to use the fractures themselves to produce energy."

"Let's see what you came up with," Power Up!'s host gestured toward a model of fissured rock layers mounted on a large table.

"Awesome! I realized if something pressure-sensitive could be slipped in, er, you know, just slipped right into those fracture crevices that would auto-fit to the space available, it could generate piezoelectric power— electricity created by pressure."

Thank God, thought Raven. At least this one can put a few sentences together. And instead of a hyper-technical gleam in his eyes, he seemed animated by good humor.

"What do you call your energy production method?" the host ad libbed.

"Fricking!" he replied with an impish grin. "'Cause, you know, you just kinda slip it in..."

Oh, snap! Raven knew the censors would blanche when they heard that on a G-rated Saturday show. But this guy was charming. Maybe they'd overlook it.

"And what materials do you use for your project?" the host tried to recover.

"I went through a lot of trial and error, but I finally determined the best material for the job-- a nano-ribbon made from a Jahn-Teller metal called grouchonium."

"Whoa! What's a Jahn-Teller metal?"

"A Jahn-Teller metal is a metal that exists in a new state of matter. You're familiar with the usual states of matter: solids, liquids and gasses, right? Well, by inserting certain metals into carbon-60 molecules known as Bucky balls, we've created metals that exist in man-made states of matter. They're hyper-durable superconductors and have other interesting characteristics."

"And grouchonium?"

"It's derived from small amounts of tellurium injected into Bucky balls. The physicist who first created that Jahn-Teller metal was a big fan of Groucho."

"Is tellurium hard to find?"

"Not really. It's a by-product of copper mining."

"So how does this produce energy?" asked the host.

"I need a zoom here!" Raven made herself heard above the studio din. A harried cameraman nodded to her.

The young man began his demonstration. "Well, you thread the nano-ribbon into the existing fissures in the rock." Tristan matched his words with deeds, moving a sinuous sliver of shiny-looking fabric through the crevices in the model's rock layers. "I made the nano-ribbon thick enough to use the natural compression from the rock. Over time, we expect rock will shift and fill in the fissures so I added an auto-adjust feature that allows the ribbon to maintain the perfect fit in between the rock layers." The young man then pushed a button that sent a crackling jolt of electricity zinging through the attached voltmeter. "It won't last forever—maybe twenty to fifty years—but while it does, the compression will generate a safe, continuous, powerful current of electricity. It makes use of existing resources – the rock crevices – and creates no pollution!" The kid looked right into the camera and made his plea. "And that's why I hope you'll vote for me and my green energy project. The $10,000 in prize money will help get us Fricking!"

Raven exhaled. No dead animals. No sludge smell. And the experiment worked! Maybe this kid was the real deal. "Cut to commercial!"

While Duluth Trading Company tried to convince viewers to buy jeans that didn't scrunch their gonads, Raven texted to friends, family and Peeps: Found a winning green energy project!

After the show on her drive home, Raven took a call from her fiancé Will.

"Hey babe," he began in that deep-chested rumbly voice that almost made her swoon.

"Are you OK? Is everything all right?"

"Let's see: It's about 5:45 in the afternoon in L.A., right?"

"Right."

"Well, it's quarter to three in the morning here in Brussels, Rave, so I'm sleepy, but I'm fine." Will didn't sound perturbed, just tired.

"So what's up?"

"I heard your text come in and ..."

"I thought you agreed to turn off your phone at night so my texts wouldn't wake you."

"Forgot. Besides, I know how important Power Up! is to you, so ...tell me about this new green energy source."

"I love you, baby. But tomorrow's another day. Go back to sleep."

"No, I'm serious. Power Up! is your dream; I want to hear all about it."

After Raven explained how electricity could be generated from a nano-ribbon slipped into existing rock fissures, Will congratulated her. But after the kudos, he added, "You know, Rave, no way the oil and gas companies are going to relinquish those fracked rocks to another energy producer. They'll want it all for themselves."

Raven swerved to avoid ramming the car ahead of her on the 405 and adjusted her Bluetooth. "Don't care; not in this to make money. I'm in it to find green energy that works. If Exxon wants to become a green energy capitalist, fine by me."

"No wonder I love you," an exhausted Army Public Relations Officer at NATO replied.

Chapter 10

Readers of the <u>Beltway Boogie</u>, <u>Huffington Post,</u> <u>Drudge Report,</u> <u>Cheezburger</u>, <u>Boing Boing</u>, <u>Politico</u>, and <u>Jezebel</u> blogs—nearly a quarter of all adults in the U.S.-- were surprised on Friday morning. Vivi hacked each of their websites and replaced the intended content of the blogs with Glenda's channeling of Thomas Paine.

American Eggs-ceptionalism

Last week citizens gathered outside the Capitol and pelted Congressional members with rotten eggs. Eighty-four percent of those polled thought Congress deserved it.

We're frustrated and angry at our government. America's profound experiment in representative democracy wobbles and teeters, struggling for oxygen.

- Why is the U.S. ranked 17 th among nations in education when we spend more money per student than any other nation?
- Why did the government bail out financial institutions to the tune of billions, but help only 1 in 10 people refinance upside down mortgages?
- Why can't veterans get the medical care they need in a timely manner? Why do we involve this country in wars unrelated to actual national security, and thus create even more veterans who need medical care?
- Why do we not require a background check before an AK-47 purchase, even after the Sandy Hook school shootings?
- Why do we spend billions on the Department of Homeland Security yet we can't keep strangers from walking in the back door of the White House?

- Why did the Supreme Court rule the way it did on Citizens United? Why is the transparency of political funding now obscured by SuperPacs?

The complicated, elusive answers all intersect in one place: Our government is no longer a strong, democratic republic, ruled by laws reflecting the will and welfare of the majority. And if we sniff around that intersection, it doesn't smell like teen spirit. It smells like money.

Is that a "D'oh!" I hear? OK, throughout history, small elite groups have ruled the many. From Roman Emperors and soldiers to nobles in the castle and serfs in the field, there have always been people who are more powerful. So, yes, we know equality is an ideal, and people have traditionally been willing to compromise. We've tolerated good monarchs, benevolent despots, and autocratic rulers as long as they don't follow the "Let them eat cake" school of thinking. Americans are angry at government not because we insist that everyone gets the same score in the game, but because we insist that the game not be rigged. And it's felt rigged for a while now.

Perhaps our anger is healthy; maybe we need to hurl eggs. A growing number of citizens are no longer content with an economic system manipulated by 1% of the population that fails the 99%. A growing number of Americans will no longer accept ultra-political correctness and Mommy-government as substitutes for common sense, moral values and reasonableness. A growing number of Americans differentiate between sensible policy discussion and the fertilizer-fests that pass for talk radio and cable news. A growing number of American citizens will no longer tolerate a Humpty Dumpty democracy.

When our frustration builds, we want to blame someone, like Congress. Or the Republicans. Or the Democrats. Or the Occupiers. Or the Tea Party. Or the Koch Brothers. Or the gays. Or Wall Street. Or immigrants. Or the ACLU. Or Olivia Pope. Or Frank Underwood.

But if we want more than emotional release, we need to bring more to the table than vitriol and a cackle berry. In a

79

representative democracy, it's up to us. If we don't own our own messes, immaturities, and ignorance, and use our collective will to correct them, the yolk's on us.

We're going to become informed, debate honestly, pay attention, and vote. We're going to use stifling bureaucratic rules to un-stifle bureaucracies. We're going to push a political agenda with humor and innovation. We're the Peeps and we're taking back our nation.

Chapter 11

All of the websites where Glenda's blog appeared kept it on the site for at least an hour before replacing it and lobbing disclaimers. In that brief period, her blog accumulated 16,702 comments-- a typical buffet served by political hacks, internet trolls, and curious citizens.

The Peeps, operating from their homes across the U.S., skimmed the numerous comments. They were pleased by the amount of interest the blog generated, all while deflecting attention from the subject of the energy bill. Glenda felt minor disappointment when she realized the majority of comments were attempts to guess her identity. She perked up again when Navya pointed out that most of the 'who wrote this' comments were from politicos; ordinary citizens cared more about the issues.

One comment in particular intrigued Emery. When the prisoners went out to the yard for their daily exercise, he found privacy in one of his chaplaincy counseling rooms. He punched Glenda's phone number into his cell.

"Glenda? Or have I reached Thomas Paine?"

Glenda recognized his voice. "Now that would be a trick, Emery. What's up?"

"Your blog has been a real blessing! Have you been following the comments?"

"Yes, yes! I love what David Brooks wrote. And did you see Nate Festring's comment?"

81

Emery could hear the excitement in her voice. "I wanted to point out one particular comment on the Cheezburger site. Scroll down past a couple hundred comments, then look for the user name SlicedRice. Do you see it?" He waited patiently for Glenda to search.

"Oh, right; here it is." She read the comment back to Emery: "'Yes, we need to do more than throw rotten eggs at those pricks in Congress. We need to make government work for everyone, not just old white billionaires. I may be in a position to help. On the down-low.' Hmm. Interesting."

"I can't explain it, Glenda, but I have an intuitive feeling that this comment is important. Do we have any way of figuring out who SlicedRice is?"

"I'll ask Vivi and see what she comes up with."

"Glad you don't think I'm being too weird about it. Anyway, good job on the blog!"

By Saturday evening, the Peeps had all talked with one another. Glenda was still feeling the adrenaline. Vivi once again crossed an uncomfortable line between legal investigation and illegal hacking, in her attempt to discover SlicedRice's identity.

"*Increible!*" Vivi began when she called Glenda. "The post originated in the White House!"

"No way!"

"*Neta*! I was hyper-careful after I realized the IP address traced to a White House server."

"A government server? At least we know it wasn't Hillary," Glenda joked.

82

Vivi laughed and continued. "This level of hacking is higher than I've handled before. So I contacted someone who knew someone. He put me in touch with a *magnifico* white-hat hacker named Einar, and he helped me take it up a notch. Several notches, really. His code is so elegant…"

"Wait, wait! Who's this Einar?" Glenda asked warily.

"A 20-year-old engineering student in Reykjavik. We Skyped; oh my god, he's so *guapo*! White blond hair and the greenest eyes! He grew up with the lead singer of Sea Bear! And he's been involved with the Open Source movement!" Clearly all of Vivi's substantial fire sizzled for this young man. "He told me how his country, Iceland, accomplished a non-violent revolution—changed its entire government and did it without firing a bullet! *Verdad*!"

"Did you tell him anything about us?"

"Only what he absolutely needed to know." Vivi paused to allow suspense to build. "Guess who posted the comment!" Before Glenda could say a word, Vivi burbled, "The President's daughter, Sarantha Peabody!"

"This is a real break for us. She could open all kinds of resources! But we'll have to be extremely careful."

"*Si*. Don't feel like celebrating my 17th birthday *en la carcel*." Vivi's brow furrowed. "I don't think our server incursion was detected. Should I give her permission to access our circle?"

"Only to our secure chat room. I've read a few articles about her; she's a troubled kid, but with her help, we'd be able to accomplish so much more."

By Monday afternoon, the President's daughter had chatted online with Raven, Ted, Glenda and Vivi. Probably because of her age, she seemed most at ease with Vivi. They'd decided to give her a basic idea of what they were trying to accomplish. When Raven told Sarantha about PowerUp! and the new green energy possibilities, the teen practically gushed. "Dad's such an incrementalist! He'll take a thousand years to put real money into green energy." She paused, considering. "I have something ... a diary my mom wrote back when she and Dad were dating. Mom tossed it in the trash years ago, but I found and kept it. Made me barf to read about my parents doing the nasty, but I think it could be useful."

"You bet it could," replied Raven, realizing that the road to green energy might be paved with x-rated journal entries.

It didn't take long for Vivi to hack into the Senate Energy bill. By replacing 'Fracking' with 'Fricking' in strategic places, she moved hundreds of thousands of dollars of research funds to the cleaner, greener cause. All the Peeps would have to do is distract Senator Lacomb on the day the bill was to be signed. As the Chair of the Energy Committee, he was the only one who would read it carefully enough to spot the "typo."

Part II: Valley Forge

Chapter 12

President Peabody recognized that the Frick/Frack typo in the new energy bill was a gift and he knew better than to look a gift horse under the tail. The Power Up! show had excited – dare he say 'energized'?- the public about Fricking. Investing in such a viable form of green energy would give America more bang for its energy buck with far less pollution. He signed the bill, making it seem as though major investment in Fricking had been the intent all along.

When President Peabody signed Senator Lacomb's Energy Bill into law, Fricking got real moolah and Navya Ghazal got real merry. She was, after all, a people person, a VP of Sales, as comfortable at a commercial real estate showing in Dubai as she was at a cocktail party in Denver. Fireworks might be premature, she thought; after all, their little revolution was just beginning. But a modest victory celebration? Absolutely! Since Navya supplied the Peeps' purse, she'd make the necessary travel and lodging arrangements.

Navya contacted Vivi Huarochiri via their secure chat room. "Wanted to check with you about where to hold our victory party. After the celebrations, we'll plan our next venture, so I figured you'll want it to be somewhere you can have cyber-security."

"*Por supuesto*, especially after we hacked the White House servers! There's a place in Big Sur. It's near an awesome beach and the motel's about as secure as you can get in this century."

"The name?"

"Deetjen's Big Sur Inn," Vivi responded. "Unless the CIA gets involved, no one's going to pick up on anything we do there. There's no wireless, not even much cell phone reception nearby."

Everyone agreed to meet at Deetjen's on the weekend in mid-September after the Energy Bill promoting Fricking was signed.

Navya had driven the California coastline numerous times. To her, Big Sur recalled hot stone massages of Ventana Spa, workshops at Esalen, and the sensual release of Namaste Bodyworks. She'd stayed in four-star hotels in Monaco, Rio, Budapest, Lisbon and Venice. She'd rented beachfront cabanas in Bali. She'd traveled the world enough to know that the vista they'd have in Big Sur was one of the best the planet had to offer.

Snuggled into a curve along California's coast, Deetjen's is a sensory meld of antique redwood buildings, white casement windows, wood smoke, creeks, vines, blossoms, and Pacific blue. Built in 1937 and modernized minimally since, Deetjen's has 'features' the way the Emperor has wardrobe: there are no TVs or phones in the rooms and no locks on the doors.

Navya rented a two-story building at Deetjen's that looked like a wolf with COPD could blow it down. The upper suite had a private deck and slept three (queen bed and a single). The lower suite had a fireplace, and a queen and two singles to sleep four. The men, Navya figured, could take the upper, leaving the first floor for the four women.

They would meet at the restaurant Friday evening for a dinner party and reconnect late Saturday afternoon to plan their next move. There'd be unstructured time after the party and before the meeting for those who wanted to hike trails, stroll the beach, or otherwise let the Big Sur vibes seep in.

Navya welcomed Raven with a hug when the Power Up! producer entered the lower suite.

Raven planted her suitcase on a twin bed and glanced at her surroundings. "Where's the TV?" She paced across the room. "Um, is this the only closet?" Raven moved to the modest bathroom. "No medicine cabinet? One towel rack?" She turned her attention from the room to Navya. "You expect four women to manage in this place? You're punkin' me, right?"

"They only had this building available. I tried to bribe them; didn't work. If Vivi hadn't insisted this was the best place to maintain a low profile, I would've looked elsewhere. I'm sorry for the inconvenience."

"I'm developing empathy for sardines." Raven could get snarky, but once she understood that security had to be more of a priority than her comfort or preferences, she shrugged her shoulders, minimized a pout, and settled in. Navya indulged in dark chocolate nougats.

Raven's reaction to the accommodations was repeated by Glenda and Ted, who showed up with a well-trimmed beard that caught Raven's attention. Vivi insisted the sacrifices of lodging luxury were necessary trade-offs for cyber-obscurity. DeVille seemed not to care much one way or the other; once he saw the woods surrounding Deetjen's, all he could talk about was chanterelle foraging. And Emery didn't mind at all. Counseling felons in a federal prison fostered gratitude for any shelter you were free to walk away from.

That evening the Peeps were seated in the restaurant at a long maple dining table. A nearby wood stove produced sweet-smelling smoke, taking the nip out of the coastal evening. Escorted by the chef, DeVille emerged from the kitchen muttering about the freshness of the food and the care with which it would be prepared. He looked, to use his word, happy.

After social chit-chat and placing orders, Raven offered a toast. "To each of you, for having the courage and desire to make America a better country. For a group of people who started out upset… ok, pissed off...at being detained at an airport, you really rose to the occasion. Thanks to you, a legitimate green energy technology has been funded. We've actually accomplished something!"

"And we got to read the underlined parts of the President's girlfriend's diary!" blurted Ted.

"Er, yes…here's to all that we've achieved. Cheers!" Raven raised her champagne glass, leading all but Vivi to do likewise. Vivi's age precluded her from the bubbly, but she'd leveled the playing field by smoking *sativa potente* before arriving.

Glenda raved about her rack of lamb. Even Vivi, whose parents were in the restaurant biz, seemed satisfied with Deetjen's fare. Once bellies were full and the third bottle of 2002 Vintage Veuve Cliquot had been uncorked, conversation quieted.

"What if the Fricking Energy Bill was our Bunker Hill?" Glenda mused.

"What do you mean?" asked Navya.

"Bunker Hill gave the colonists a false sense of how easy it would be to fight the British. Not every piece of legislation will pass as easily as the Energy bill."

The Peeps were tired from their travels and didn't much care about the nuances of Revolutionary War history. The group agreed to meet the next day at 3 PM to plan their agenda. The victory party wrapped, with murmured reflections and two fizzy burps.

Emery, DeVille, and Ted retreated to the upper suite, the unit shared by the Peeps men. Ted and Emery offered the single bed to DeVille because of his size.

Ted took an after-dinner walk along the coastal highway, watching moonlight spatter on Pacific surf. When he returned to the complex, he retrieved his acoustic guitar from the trunk of his rental car, and sat down to play on a wooden bench near their unit. Raven heard the music and came out of the cramped female quarters to get some fresh air. At least that's what she told herself.

Ted set his capo for a melancholy rendition of the Band Perry's "If I Die Young." He strummed and sang softly, almost whispering. Visitors to Deetjen's liked quiet.

There was enough space on the bench for Raven to sit next to Ted, but she stood, moving slightly with the music.

"*...Sink me in a river at dawn...*"

Not my jam, she thought, but damn, he was good.

"*...Send me away with the words of a love song...*"

When he finished, she walked over and nudged him on the shoulder. "You're pretty good, ya know." She crinkled her nose. "I mean, for a conservative," she added.

Ted grinned like every one of his country western music heroes and looked her up and down. "I think you're okay, too." He offered the guitar to her. "You play?"

"No way," Raven laughed. "But I wouldn't mind listening to another song before I turn in for the night."

Ted stood and stretched, showing off his lean, hard build. When he sat back down, he stroked his new beard as he contemplated which song to sing. In a baritone whisper, he crooned, *"And I'd give up forever to touch you/ 'Cause I know that you feel me somehow,"* a phonic pheromone.

Emery had flown into San Jose airport early for the Peeps meeting, allowing himself time beforehand to visit a Monterey historical site – a Methodist Episcopal church retreat popular in the 1880s. But historical church sites weren't the only thing he was checking out. For years he'd been praying about his attraction to men, reading liberation theology, and working up the nerve to have an encounter. In the two years he'd been married decades ago, he'd had sex with his wife exactly three times and each time had been as erotic as watching C-span. He wasn't sure he was gay, but he was certain he wasn't heterosexual.

After the Peeps victory dinner, Emery drove his rental car 30 miles back to Monterey where he sought out a pub listed in a Gay Men's Guide to California. The pub smelled of beer and yeast, fish and chips, fog and ocean. He hadn't been there more than ten minutes when a neatly bearded man in jeans and a peach-colored sweatshirt walked in and sat near him at the bar. Emery took in the fellow's carriage, his solid core, the physicality that spoke of hours in the gym. Emery also appreciated the man's teal-colored eyes.

After ordering a Green Flash IPA, the man nodded in Emery's direction and said, "Name's Matt, Matt Sandstone."

"Emery Palmer." He reached out and shook Matt's hand. "I'm from Portland. Visiting Big Sur with some friends. You?"

Matt's whole face lit up. "I live in Seattle! My sister lives here. She just had a baby, my first nephew, so I came to visit."

Emery's heart did all the things hearts were supposed to do in cheap romance novels. Surely if God gave him such feelings, it wouldn't be sinful to act on them. "What do you do in Seattle?"

Matt's expression turned sheepish. He lowered his head slightly and answered, "I run the Washington State office of the Log Cabin Republicans." He took a long swallow of his beer as Emery processed that. "I don't usually share that right away; it complicates my dating life." He shifted uncomfortably on his bar stool. "What do you do?"

"I'm a Methodist minister," Emery said. "Definitely complicates *my* dating life."

Matt chortled. "Let me buy you a drink, preacher man!"

Saturday Morning.

Glenda took deep breaths. Flowering shrubs, wood smoke and ocean salt scented the air. An early riser, she'd managed to slip out of the women's suite without waking her fellow Peeps. She continued her walk through morning fog along the Coastal Highway until she reached the Henry Miller Memorial Library. The place intrigued Glenda. After all, she'd spent a good chunk of her adolescence reading and rereading *Tropic of Capricorn*. The sign in the window said it didn't open until 11; she'd have to return later. She reversed direction, returning to Deetjen's on the Pacific side of the road as gulls harbingered the day. She paused and breathed deeply, feeling fully alive, wishing she believed in God so she'd have someone to thank for the day.

Ted and Vivi finished their ascent and reached the trail crest where they admired the view. In the distance below them, McWay Falls sprayed an 80-foot column of mist and foam as it emptied directly into the Pacific from a nearby state park. The day was almost too perfect. The fog had burned off; all was brilliant sun, blue sky, mild breeze and early burnish on autumn leaves. Ted had joined the teen on her hike when he noticed her heading off alone. You never knew what kind of weirdos could be hiding out in the California wilderness; he wanted to keep a protective eye on her. Ted offered Vivi his water canteen.

She took a long drink and considered her hike companion. At least Ted was fit; he'd made it up the trail without huffing and puffing. She wanted to Skype her new love interest Einar; none of these old fart Peeps was much fun. Only Raven spoke Spanish, and not one of them knew how to code even a basic mobile app, something she could do in seventh grade. #clueless!

She felt distant from the Peeps in some ways, but there was an undeniable sense of adventure about their 'revolution.' It was like someone had said she could not only sit at the grownup's blackjack table; she could deal, ante, bet, and win or lose. Vivi knew her hacking skills were essential to the Peeps; she also knew it was likely she'd be caught. Not everyone had as much Teflon with legal authorities as Snowden. She knew enough about the world to realize that accomplishing something that mattered didn't happen often. She would stay at this blackjack table as long as she could.

Vivi took another swallow and returned Ted's canteen. She reached into the side pocket of her camo pants and offered him candy from her prized Sponge Bob Pez dispenser. The view of the waterfalls touched her. If this venture ended with a long prison sentence, she may never see such sights again.

Raven sipped her margarita and surveyed the open blue horizon from the patio of Café Keva, part of the Nepenthe Inn complex, which also included a restaurant, bar and gift shop, all perched cliffside as close to the ocean as you could get without a wet suit. She loved just sitting there, letting her self-discipline and ambition off-leash, allowing the warm sun to relax her. A honeybee, unusual this far into September, buzzed a nearby vine. This whole endeavor may be crazy, she thought, but look what we've accomplished! A promising new source of green energy is now well-funded. I can survive Deetjen's; I'll schedule myself a nice massage before I leave. She sipped and let the blended lime ice prickle her taste buds. Ted had a nice baritone. Dawg had him some sugar buns, too. Why the hell did he have to be one of these Tea Party types? Maybe I miss Will more than I realize.

Raven's eyes followed a red tail hawk searching for prey. Her own thoughts took sinuous turns. Before Power Up!, I was a reporter, not a producer. I thought like a reporter. I think differently now. If I didn't, why… What a scoop the Peeps would make! A group of seemingly normal citizens hacking and manipulating Congressional legislation to throw a second American Revolution? My story would be on every news show; my reputation would soar! Like that hawk, like that smoothly circling hawk.

After a while Raven drifted into the nearby gift shop. She was browsing high-end eclectic wares when she spied Navya to her right in the clothing section. Navya was looking in a mirror, holding a bold yellow silk tunic in front of her, trying to determine if the color was right for her skin tone. When Navya spotted Raven, she began switching between the yellow tunic in her right hand and a turquoise blouse in her left, back and forth, each held under her chin in turn, inviting Raven's opinion. The overall effect was of a plump referee signaling illegal motion fouls with floral bouquets.

Later when they departed the gift shop, Raven gestured toward the blue Pacific. "My fiancé Will is stationed at NATO headquarters in Brussels. When he returns, I want to bring him here. It's romantic, don't you think? Maybe you and your husband would enjoy some time here, too."

Navya scanned the broad expanse of marine blue. "Perhaps. But I doubt we'll stay at Deetjen's."

DeVille had bonded so successfully with Deetjen's chef, Emilio, that his new friend allowed him to season that night's cassoulet. DeVille entered the kitchen carrying a basket of chanterelles, delighting his fellow foodie. He began meticulously mincing garlic, parsley, and thyme, added whole cloves, and swaddled it all in cheesecloth for a bouquet garni.

Glad to have such capable help, Emilio asked him, "What happened to you in Vietnam? To your head, I mean... if you don't mind talking about it."

DeVille's huge frame had been bent over while he worked on the seasonings. At Emilio's question, he stood up straight and looked the younger man in the eyes. DeVille saw a 30-year-old bright, hard-working young man maybe a bit too soft in the underbelly. DeVille considered, then began his story. "I was a cook at the Marine compound near the Phu Bai air base. Ever hear of it?" He paused, shifting his weight from one side to the other.

"No, man. Can't say I have."

"Happened January 30th. The Viet Cong launched an attack; later the papers called it the Battle of Hué. I was 20 years old. A kid." He laid a chef's knife on the counter. "And at 20, most important thing to me was girls. Know what I mean?"

Emilio grinned. "I do know what you mean!"

"I was seein' this local shopkeeper's daughter." DeVille washed his hands at the sink. "She was 16. Her name was Tuyen, means angel. She treated me like an angel." He drew inward and allowed the memory to pierce. "I think she liked me 'cause I'd bring food for her family when I visited." DeVille winced. "These non-slip floors hurt my feet after a while."

Emilio hustled a stool from a supply closet and set it nearby. "Here, rest."

DeVille uttered a fu-jingle-mingle-tingle softly and continued. "That day—January 30th-- we caught all hell from the VC-- rockets, grenades, mortar fire. My Staff Sergeant ordered me out to the air base to help unload provisions. I didn't want to go. I mean, I really didn't want to go. Had some kinda premonition about it, cher."

The younger chef nodded.

"But the sooner the provisions were unloaded, the sooner I could sneak some food to Tuyen and her family. So I went. Next thing I know, piece of shrapnel cracks through my skull and slices my brain open. I dropped this big carton of canned pears I was carrying. Can't eat canned pears to this day. I fell on the tarmac and laid there till a corpsman reached me. Emilio, everything went through my busted up mind -- the smell of my mother's skin lotion. The sound of the church bell in my old neighborhood. The feel of my first dog's coat; little black and white terrier named Tiggy. And fear... you see I'm a pretty big dude, right?"

Emilio nodded. "Sure, man. You gotta be, what? Six-four?"

DeVille nodded. "Well, let me tell you, cher – big men get scared, too. Least this big man did." He took a long, deep breath and whispered his mantra. "I didn't really feel a lot of pain. Maybe I was in shock, don't know. But so much blood poured outta my head I was sure I was gonna die. Last thing I remembered was the image of my father's key ring. Had a rabbit's foot on it."

For several moments, DeVille sat silently on the stool, lost in memories. Emilio prompted him, "What happened then?"

"This part of me," DeVille tapped his head, "checked out. Woke up in a hospital in Saigon with a scar on my skull. They opened my head up like a Zip Loc bag and closed it again." After a few moments, DeVille stood again, lifted the pot lid from the cassoulet, and inhaled deeply. He gave a nod of approval to Emilio. "Don't remember much else about it."

Emilio said, "Sorry you had to go through that, man. I'm surprised you still work. You could've claimed disability, right?"

DeVille looked out the kitchen window and watched several of his Peeps companions come into the restaurant for lunch before their meeting. "Could've, yes. But I wanted to be happy."

Saturday –Meeting Time

Square footage was at a premium inside the lower suite. Peeps shoved suitcases and pillows to clear a spot on beds; early arrivals got chairs and struck up a game of hearts while waiting. Emery was the last to arrive, and everyone noticed that he looked 50 Shades of Gay. As in happy, that is.

Raven couldn't help herself. "What's up? Ted said you didn't get in till really late last night. Figured you'd be tired and grouchy today, but you look like a kid at Disneyland."

"All right, all right; you might as well know." Emery rubbed his chin and looked around the room with a goofy grin. "For years, I've wrestled with whether or not I was gay. Last night, I discovered I am!" The news was met with decided indifference, leading Emery to deduce they didn't fully appreciate the significance of what he was sharing. "For a clergy person in a denomination that struggles with the issue, coming out is no small thing. But last night was...wow, definitely a blessing! Wish I'd had the courage to face who I am a long time ago."

After a few seconds of silence, Ted said, "Glad we only shared a bed *half* the night last night. Might've ruined my reputation." The sparkle in his eyes and humor in his voice conveyed a good-natured acceptance not many expected of the Tea Partyer.

Vivi burst out singing Lady Gaga's *Born This Way*, without too many Spanglish flourishes. Raven joined in, but the singing trailed off when Glenda smoothed her eyebrows and got down to business. "OK, our next goal is legislation that will introduce more common sense and efficiency to federal regulations. We called it 'Make Regulation Make Sense,' remember?"

Ted rubbed his hands together eagerly. "This is my puppy; can't wait!"

"Me, too! Businesses will surge!" Navya added.

"You were going to list some principles; things you believe could make federal regulation more sensible, right?" Glenda prompted Ted.

"For sure!" Ted handed out photocopies of a list he'd typed. "Here you go." When everyone had a copy, he began. "Most government agencies can't respond to our needs because they're choked with bureaucratic red tape." He shifted his weight, looked around the room and continued. "They're like cars with clogged air filters. Nothing wrong with the engine, nothing wrong with the gas. But try to drive, and the engine sputters and stalls out on you. The engine can't get the air it needs to mix with fuel for combustion." Ted looked at Raven, raised an eyebrow suggestively and said, "We all want a little combustion in our life, don't we?"

When Raven ignored him, Ted continued. "If the air filter's clogged, things can't flow right. Same for government agencies. Too many regs and the good things agencies are supposed to do can't flow right. I'm sure you're all aware of how many roads and bridges need repair; how many good and worthwhile infrastructure projects are snagged in regs that no one has the power to deal with. And remember a while back, the head of the DEA testified before Congress that, due to civil service regs, she couldn't fire the asshats who hired prostitutes on the job?" Ted shifted his weight, looked up from the handout, and checked the faces of his fellow Peeps. "OK, so here's what I came up with. Number 1. When a project requires approval from any federal agency or agencies, one person and one person only will be the ultimate decision-maker. The buck will stop there. Number 2. If more than one federal agency is required to approve a project, one agency has to take the lead and be responsible for coordinating with all other federal agencies to move the project forward. Number 3. Every regulation on the books for certain federal agencies…" Ted looked up from his notes to his co-conspirators. "I picked the ones that screw up most in the eyes of ordinary citizens—the V.A., Homeland Security, the EPA, TSA, and the Office of Personnel Management." Before Glenda could ask him, he added, "I took an informal poll at a BBQ last month." He returned to the handout and continued. "Where was I? Oh, right… Last but not least, every reg on the books for these agencies will be given a common sense review and a sunset review by a committee of ordinary citizens, drawn randomly from a pool, just like juries."

"That's a tall order, Ted, and an impressive one. Big federal agencies have thousands of regulations. How will ordinary citizens know enough to evaluate these regs meaningfully?" Glenda asked.

"I thought we'd get the help of second and third-year law students. Maybe the students could get school credit for serving on regs committees. Their job would be to translate legalese into plain English so that the appointed citizens can understand the regs. The common sense review will determine whether the reg makes sense; the sunset review will decide whether the regulation should be phased out eventually, and if so, when."

"If we pull this off, Ted, America's economy is going to fly! I am definitely on board." All smiles, Navya passed around a salver of gourmet fudge.

Raven turned toward Glenda. "What are the politics of getting this approved by Congress?"

"With a Republican President and a Republican majority in the House, it shouldn't be too hard. The Senate has a Democratic majority; that will be harder. The Dems may want to exempt the EPA."

"No," Ted asserted. "No exemptions for the EPA; they're one of the worst offenders!"

Faces with troubled expressions turned toward Ted. Raven asked, "Ted, how can you be in Big Sur, surrounded by such natural beauty, and not feel that the environment is worth protecting?"

"I want a clean natural environment. But we humans are native to the planet, too. We have as much right to feed, clothe, shelter and entertain ourselves as any other species. We have the right to farm, build, and otherwise use the earth… as long as we respect it. Some of the EPA's regulations are insane! I mean, they'll hold up an otherwise good project, like a new neighborhood school, or repairing a bridge, all because the Litmus Blue Aerie Fairy Caterpillar may become extinct. You know, stuff like that. I mean, do you feel bad about life because you never got to pet a dodo?"

Navya was loving this. "What's good for the D-O-D-O is good for the E-P-A!"

Emery spoke up. "I'm not sure I can support any agenda that destroys the environment. It's threatened enough already by climate change. According to my beliefs, God created us as caretakers of the planet."

"Besides," Raven prodded, "what if the Litmus Blue Aerie Fairy Caterpillar produced a chemical that healed burn wounds or prevented heart attacks?"

"Thought of that," said Ted. "If any species is threatened when EPA regs change –not saying any would be, but in that worst-case scenario – I'd include something in our legislation that requires the DNA of any endangered species to be stored by the…" Ted glanced at his notes and continued. "… American Museum of Natural History. They've got a liquid nitrogen storage bank. I looked it up. They're kind of a Noah's Ark for species preservation."

"It's not your intention to gut the EPA, is it?" Emery asked.

Ted responded quickly. "Doesn't matter whether I, personally, would gut the EPA or not. The point is to make sure someone with common sense reviews federal regulations, according to the wisdom of everyday Americans." Here he turned to Glenda with a meaningful nod. "We either want real democracy or we don't. I'm willing to trust the American people. If their common sense says only ten regs are necessary instead of 100, great. If they say a 100 are needed, so be it."

Tension filled the Peeps, and the suite grew silent for a moment. Emery and Vivi took bathroom breaks. Finally DeVille stood up. He recited a few fu-jingle-mingle-tingles to center himself, and spoke. "Behind my house in New Orleans, I have a garden. I grow leeks, onions, basil, okra… Made the best damned gumbo last summer with my okra, cher. Oh, and I grow beans, sage, rosemary, the juiciest melons. And spinach. Sometimes tomatoes, although the bugs usually find 'em before I do." Several of the Peeps thought DeVille had lost the drift of the conversation, but he surprised them. "I love my garden; it makes me happy! But I'd hate to think what that garden would look like if I never weeded it." He paused. "I go to a VA Medical Center for care, and I can tell you, lot of weeds growing in the V.A. And at the Civil Service office, the EPA, places like that. Makes sense they need a good weeding."

The sky had clouded over and large rain drops spattered the redwood siding of their unit. Several Peeps were shivering. Ted kindled a fire in the fireplace. Eventually Glenda steered them back to the work at hand. "It should be fairly easy to get a prominent Republican to sponsor this 'better regs' bill. Does anyone know Representative Cannon?"

"I know Cannon," Navya volunteered. "Why?"

"He chairs the House Committee on Government Oversight and Reform. It would be a great place for a regs bill to originate."

"I was a major donor to his last reelection campaign," Navya said. "I can arrange a one-on-one with him. He'd probably love to sponsor this bill!"

Glenda seemed pleased. "Good. I'll reach out to grass roots organizations trying to revise government regulations. I may even be able to create support among construction worker unions. Infrastructure investment has clearly been stalled by government regs. It's a massive project, Ted, and it will irk some people. You can count on that. But my sense is the country's ready for a good Spring cleaning. Let's do it." Glenda offered one of her rare smiles.

After more planning and a touch of schmoozing, the Peeps called it a day.

"I'm in," said Raven, winking at Ted. "But before I check out tomorrow, I'll hike the trails in search of a Litmus Blue Aerie Fairy Caterpillar … before it's too late."

Chapter 13

President Basho Samuels Peabody started his day with two slices of toast slathered with almond butter, the *Wall Street Journal*, the *Washington Post*, and a monstrous mug of coffee. The Journal's headline was "Exxon and Mobil Invest in 16 Fricking Sites." The Post had a smaller front page article, "Fricking Tech Firm Leads NASDAQ in Gains." Big Oil was Fricking delighted. Now that they knew how profitable it was, the oil and gas industry had become Fricking's biggest proponents. This was good news for Peabody, who needed support from Big Oil's lapdog, Senator Lacomb, to get his tax reform proposal passed. He'd meet with him this afternoon.

He checked his daily calendar. After the National Security Briefing, he would sign a Presidential proclamation making December 30th National Bacon Day. While not a national priority, it would appease certain right-wingers in his party who frowned upon celebrating National Bacon Day on International Bacon Day, which fell near Labor Day. After all, why should the American celebration yield to the Danish or the Australians? Damn, all this thinking about bacon made him crave it. Somehow almond butter toast didn't offer the same satiation.

His bacon proclamation would be followed by lunch and the meeting with Senator Lacomb. After Lacomb, there'd be a brief meeting with a handful of grassroots protesters advocating for some cause on the government's We, the People petition site. He'd instructed his Chief of Staff to squeeze in a meeting with petitioners at least once a week. He would wrap his day with a State dinner with Vladimir Putin.

Director of National Intelligence David Nirvidian plunked two sugar cubes in his morning tea and began the daily "President's Eyes Only" security briefing. Every time he paused between paragraphs, he licked his lips, a nervous habit from years of bugle practice as a child.

Peabody, sitting across from Nirvidium in the Oval Office, reviewed the brief. "Russian incursion into Mongolia? What do the Mongolians have that Putin wants?"

"Fricking is dependent on the manufacture of nano-ribbons which utilizes a by-product of copper mining. Mongolia has some of the world's largest remaining copper deposits." He sipped his tea. "Russian shell corporations have purchased majority holdings in several Chilean copper mines. We think Putin's trying to corner the market."

"Why doesn't Russia use the same approach in Mongolia as they're doing in Chile?"

"Chile's a signatory of the Rio Pact, the Inter-American Treaty of Reciprocal Assistance. Mongolia isn't. State says we haven't signed any treaties that would obligate us to defend Mongolia if Putin invades."

"Will he?"

"Our sources in Ulaan Baatar and communication intercepts from Moscow indicate he'll be aggressive in arm-twisting and back-room deals, but that his implied threat of invasion is bluster. A strategy, not a tactic."

"Recommendations?"

"We need to amp up Mongolian intel. A bit of creative communication with Beijing may help. China owns mineral rights to several of the copper mines Russia covets."

"I'll authorize the additional intel resources. Let's keep a close eye on this." President Peabody skimmed the rest of the daily briefing. His eyes had almost reached the bottom of the final page when David Nirvidian cleared his throat.

"Mr. President, there's another matter I just received word of a few minutes before our meeting. It's not in the brief."

"Yes?"

"You've followed the briefings about the homegrown militia build-up in Georgia and the Carolinas?"

Peabody nodded.

"Last night, three National Guard armories in North Carolina were burglarized. No one's been harmed, but thousands of weapons have been stolen."

"You suspect these militia groups?"

"Let me put it this way, Mr. President. These homegrown militias have almost acquired enough assault rifles, rocket launchers, anti-tank weapons, incendiary devices, bullet-proof vests, and ammunition to open their own National Guard armory. And many of these militia members are veterans. They have buddies in the military, including the National Guard --- buddies whose duty it might be to guard armories."

"Arrange for several of our best people to review camera surveillance of the military armories on the dates of the burglaries; see if we can confirm that these militia groups are stealing the weapons. And talk to the Pentagon about doubling the number of armory guards on bases in the South. We have to nip this in the bud." Peabody looked at David. "I know the good old boys down South like their guns, but this warrants caution. Is there anything in particular going on in Georgia or the Carolinas I should know about?"

Despite the depressing crap he had to deal with, his National Intelligence Director had retained his sense of humor. "We're keeping an eye on them," David replied. "If they start gathering vats of moonshine for a big block party, we'll bust them before the party gets out of hand."

"How sure are we about the intelligence on Putin from Mongolia?"

David Nirvidian shrugged his shoulders. He'd learned that nothing, particularly in intelligence work, is certain. "Intelligence from the ground has been confirmed by communication intercepts."

"Well, it'll keep the conversation lively at tonight's State dinner."

Basho Samuels Peabody took a few minutes after the security briefing to stretch his legs. He followed the path from the Oval Office in the direction of the Rose Garden. His peripheral vision detected movement. He scanned and caught a glimpse of long blond hair between the rose bushes. The President stood still and observed his daughter Sarantha crouch between a dark Queen Elizabeth *grandiflora* and a pale tea rose. She reached for the velvety

Queen Elizabeth and pulled the stem towards her, scraping the inside of her left forearm with its thorns. Several crimson dots emerged. She stopped crouching, stood up and focused on the thin rivulets of blood dripping down her arm. While it hurt to see his daughter do any self-harm, what struck him was how minor the damage was compared to what she'd been doing a few months ago.

After signing the bacon proclamation, President Peabody had lunch. Between bites of his BLT, he read position papers, situational analyses, advisories, State Department guidance for his dinner with Putin, and political cartoons. He then returned to the Oval Office where his Chief of Staff greeted him. "Senator Lacomb is waiting for you."

Lacomb stood and shook Peabody's hand when the President entered the room.

"Thanks for coming. Please, have a seat." President Peabody sat down across from Lacomb, rather than distance himself behind the Oval Office desk. "Henry, I was a bit hard on you regarding that matter with the diary. Although the note that accompanied it said it was from your daughter, the FBI and Secret Service never found any fingerprints or trace forensics from her, or from anyone else for that matter. And of course, she's never run any of that material in her blog. Must've been someone's idea of a joke. At any rate, through a twist of fate, it did bring Fricking into the US economy, which I'm sure your friends at Big Oil fully appreciate."

Lacomb offered a curdled smile. "We made lemonade from lemons tossed in the garbage."

"Careful or some reporter will say you support a national compost program."

Lacomb shifted in his chair. "With all due respect, enough bullshit about compost," he said with no apparent irony. "Why did you call this meeting?"

"Have you heard about the new "Make Regulation Make Sense" bill introduced in the House by Cannon, a Congressman from San Diego?"

Lacomb's brow cleared and his voice grew more enthusiastic. "Heard a few things. A major overhaul of agency regulations, right? I'd love it, the business world would love it, and the Republican Party would love it. But it'll never make it through a Democratic Senate."

"You're one of the most powerful legislative brokers in either chamber. And I'll throw the entire weight of the Presidency into getting this new regulations bill passed. Are you telling me it can't be done?"

"Well, a few of the more moderate Democrats might...hmm. It would take some arm wrestling," Lacomb hem-hawed. "Maybe I could talk to...."

"You know you have the clout, Henry. You can do this. We can put your name on the bill. Your pals in Oil and Gas will reward your efforts." Contemplating deregulation inspired in Lacomb visions of sugar plum-y deposits to his investment accounts. Peabody knew he had him hooked. He continued his strategy. "So, I'll use the bully pulpit as much as possible to support the regulations bill. But I need you to do something for me, too."

Senator Lacomb frowned. He hadn't seen the quid pro quo coming. "And what would that be?" he asked skeptically.

"I'd like to know why you won't back my tax reform bill. I've linked tax breaks proportionately to capital investment and job creation. Our country needs this. It will promote more networks, consortia, and other public-private partnerships." Peabody moved from the chair across from Lacomb and sat behind the Resolute desk. "Are you against it simply because your bosom buddy," Peabody let sarcasm drip all over that term, "Nate Festring, is against it? Or do you have any actual issues with it, Henry?"

"You removed every tax write-off for oil and gas exploration and for capital investments in the Energy Industry!"

'Energy Industry' was Lacomb-speak for Big Oil. At last President Peabody realized what was bugging Lacomb. "You honestly want me to continue tax breaks for gas and oil when they're making money hand over fist with Fricking which costs them almost nothing?"

"Yes."

"That's crazy, Senator."

"I don't see it that way. Until the major capital investment tax write-offs are restored, I won't support your tax reform bill."

Peabody stood and walked across the Oval Office to gaze out a window. He pondered how to respond to such idiotic crap. He seriously did not like this guy Lacomb. When he finally returned his attention to the senator, all he said was, "Thanks for coming by, Henry. We'll talk again soon."

Moments later, Chief of Staff Roger Shellish entered. "Mr. President, time for your meeting with a grassroots delegation from the We, the People government petition website."

"I read the summary you provided on their petition, but I want to be sure I understand. These people are petitioning the government to ban pig wrestling? With everything else going on in this country, pig wrestling is their major concern?"

"Yes, Mr. President." Roger's eyes twinkled with humor. "You instructed me to select a grassroots petition each week; you wanted to meet with real citizens. The petition for this week is to ban pig wrestling based on its cruelty. It's supported by the ASPCA, the Animal Legal Defense Fund, and by Eckhardt over in Agriculture."

"I'll tell you what's cruel, Roger – having me declare National Bacon Day when I'm so full of compassion for pigs!" Though his words sounded like a complaint, Shellish knew Peabody relished the bizarre humor.

At the State dinner that evening, Peabody looked Russian Premier Putin in the eyes. He failed to see the honest amigo "W" had seen. To Peabody, Putin's face offered all the warmth of the Eye of Sauron. When Putin swallowed his last bite of rib eye, Peabody leaned toward him and the interpreter. Simply and clearly he said, "Move on Mongolia, and you'll give me common ground with Beijing. I'll ensure every U. S. contract for copper goes to Chile, Canada, China or Mexico."

After the State dinner during a photo op handshake, the ex-KGB officer squeezed Peabody's hand in a demonstration of machismo. He hadn't done that during their initial greeting; he waited until the reporters' cameras were clicking before he proffered his death grip.

When affairs of state wrapped that evening, Peabody visited the White House kitchen and put in a special request with the baker. Before Putin departed the next morning, a Presidential aide offered the Russian a box of warm, aromatic pastries to enjoy on his flight home. Peabody affixed a note to the package: "Your handshake grip yesterday evoked the strength of a Russian bear. Americans call these pastries Bear Claws. I thought you might enjoy them."

The baker had combined almond paste, sugar, salt, butter, egg whites, and almond flavoring into puff pastry, along with one additional ingredient specially requested by the President: a mega-dose of Metamucil.

Chapter 14

The President's calendar was packed. He'd had his national security briefing and his weekly lunch with the Vice President. He'd awarded the Medal of Honor to a Marine who'd lost his vision in Afghanistan, and he'd discussed the new end-of-third-quarter numbers with various players from his economic team.

In late afternoon just when Peabody thought he might catch a few minutes of unstructured time, Roger Shellish rushed in, out of breath, looking more concerned than Peabody had ever seen him.

"Mr. President, I need to speak with you privately. It's urgent!"

"Do I need the nuclear code book?"

"No, no. Not that kind of urgent. But it's urgent."

Peabody led him into his private office and closed the door behind them. "Out with it, Roger."

"OK," the Chief of Staff caught his breath and began. "Remember when there was an incursion on the White House servers back in August and the FBI investigated?"

Peabody nodded.

"They never came up with evidence that could be used in court, but the security breach was linked to a teenage girl in Texas, Vivi Huarochiri. She's been associated with Edward Snowden, WikiLeaks, and Anonymous."

"A teenager? Has she been recruited by the Chinese? The Russians?"

"No, nothing like that, sir. The FBI set up surveillance on the girl in hopes she'd slip up. They've monitored all of her computer activities." Roger took a deep breath and prepared to give the President news he really didn't want to hear. "Through this young woman, we think Sarantha has been integrated into a group of rebel citizens who want to affect a second American revolution. They call themselves the Peeps."

"The Peeps?"

"As in 'We, the Peeps.' Yes, sir. I requested that the FBI classify the reports on the White House server breach at the highest possible security clearance, and only speak to you, David Nirvidian, or me about it."

"Is this that group of pig-lovers I met with? From the We, the People government petition site?"

"Don't think so, sir. It seems to be a small citizens group interested in big things like green energy and income inequality."

"But why involve Sarantha? Are they trying to gain leverage on me or the government? Do they want to brainwash her, make her the Manchurian President's daughter? What?"

"We don't know as much as we'd like to, sir. The young woman whom we suspect breached our servers is a

115

sophisticated hacker, and she knows other hackers who help cover her tracks. The Peeps themselves seem to be ordinary people trying to accomplish a non-violent second American revolution. And for some reason – and I don't think it's malicious – they've included your daughter in their ranks. In fact, it seems more like she inserted herself into their group through a comment she left on a blog. They did not seek her out, at least there's no evidence to that effect."

The President's face showed relief. His daughter wasn't being held hostage or threatened. "How large is this group?"

"Seven people, sir, not including Sarantha."

"Hmm. A non-violent second American revolution? Like to know how a mere handful of people plan to pull that one off."

"They may be non-violent, Mr. President, but they're not exactly lawful. So far your daughter seems only minimally involved. Nevertheless, I thought you should know immediately."

"Yes, of course." The President sorted this new information in his mind. He thought of Sarantha, of the cutting, of her disinterest in everything he suggested. Yet somehow these Peeps had reached something in her, something that wanted to be involved in their cause. "Make certain only one or two trustworthy agents work on this. I'd like background checks of each person in this group, basically any info we have on them that's relevant."

The Chief of Staff raised an eyebrow.

Peabody clarified, "By relevant I mean I don't want some crap J. Edgar Hoover put together about their father or grandfather smoking weed at the '68 convention."

"Of course, sir."

"Thank you for your discretion in this matter."

Shellish departed in a much calmer mood than when he'd arrived.

Peabody stayed in his private office for a while, remembering the 2-year-old who wouldn't stop giggling in her bubble bath. He remembered the 4-year-old who found seagull feathers at the beach and blew puffs at them to make them soar again. He remembered the 7-year-old's gray eyes wide with awe when she met her great-great uncle, an Algonquian shaman, who presented her with a handmade ancestral pendant. And Peabody definitely remembered the tears shed at 10 when she realized her mother was leaving to work with Doctors Without Borders and she would be left behind…with him.

The President selected the number for his daughter's therapist on his personal cell. He reached her voice mail. "Dr. Henigson, there's something I'd like to discuss with you about my daughter. Please return my call as soon as possible." He paused then quickly added, "If you didn't recognize my voice, this is the President."

After she'd returned his call and they'd consulted on the issue, Peabody once more summoned his Chief of Staff. "Clear my schedule for this coming weekend, Roger. I want to invite a special guest to Camp David."

On the helicopter ride to Camp David, President Peabody studied the profiles of the citizens group who called themselves the Peeps. Four names were listed as members; three as suspected members. They lived all over the country, apparently having connected at Logan International when all were wrongfully detained by security. Peabody recalled the incident; it had led to firing the TSA's Administrator. None seemed the type of person who would harm his daughter. Their background checks revealed nothing significant, although DeVille Tiamante had had a charge of possession of less than an ounce of marijuana, and Vivi Huarochiri had crossed the line a few times in her involvement with WikiLeaks. She was a 16-year-old kid, barely older than Sarantha, with no history of violence and an uncle in the diplomatic corps. The more Peabody learned, the more hopeful he felt about the situation.

Sarantha's therapist had agreed that this might be the opportunity his daughter needed to develop a sense of self not dependent on a mother who'd left her or on a father whose political role obscured her.

"Smartasses!" thought Mohiinok, elder shaman of the Winooku, the Algonquian tribe from which President Peabody's Native American ancestors hailed. When Mohiinok stood as straight as his aged spine would allow, he was almost five feet four inches tall. His face offered a labyrinth of wrinkles and crinkles. His eyes were like obsidian, and he wore his silver hair in a pony tail. Mohiinok looked at least a century old, but no one really knew.

Secret Service agents had arrived at the reservation to whisk him off to Camp David in a Presidential jet.

Because he took time to consider and did not always respond immediately to their questions or comments, the agents thought him stupid or senile. Knowing they didn't speak Winooku, the shaman had begun referring to them as Lard Butt and Hard Head in his language. It provided an interior chuckle and helped him cope with their arrogance. It was clear they didn't think much of having to spend a weekend escorting an ancient Native American who insisted on bringing a pipe that reeked of marijuana onto a government flight.

Mohiinok liked the grand-nephew who'd summoned him. He'd met him several times when Peabody was young. His character flaw at the time had been a certain lack of ambition. How the hell this particular nephew got to be President was a mystery only the great Manitou could answer. Mohiinok realized Peabody hadn't spent any real time with him in almost 40 years. His grand-nephew wouldn't know if he was smart or senile, wise or merely wizened. The concept of a shaman elder to folks who grew up in the white man's world would be some guru issuing the occasional monosyllabic grunt interpreted as profound. Or a shriveled elder tripping on psychedelic vision quests. In truth Mohiinok was a deep and playful soul, ready to hear the owl call his name but not yet yearning for that call. In his shamanic practice, he'd visited other realms many times, knew they existed, and he didn't fear death. That allowed him to take things less seriously. He would try to help his nephew, but he might tease a bit while doing so.

Before he left the reservation, he'd put word out through tribal connections that he'd be visiting Camp David. Near the border between western Maryland and Pennsylvania, the Presidential facility was in Algonquian territory. Certain members of his people maintained surveillance on the place and were often on the grounds

119

without being detected by the Secret Service. Night vision goggles and signal jammers were available to Native Americans, too. You never knew when intelligence about Camp David might be useful.

Mohiinok looked through the jet's window as they approached. Hard Head and Lard Butt might not approve, but he was looking forward to the adventure.

Hours later Peabody sat in the Camp David den with Mohiinok. The shaman sat on the floor and loaded a ceremonial pipe with a blend of cannabis sativa, damiana, wild lettuce, sage, tobacco, and dragonfly wings. Peabody wasn't sure whether Mohiinok was screwing with him about the dragonfly wings, but if Mohiinok smoked this and lived all these years, whatever they were inhaling probably wasn't harmful.

The elder inhaled deeply, coughed, and offered the pipe to his great-nephew. "This house has the stink of power."

"It'll stink of more than power after this." Peabody was enjoying the smoke. His mind had become so agitated by Putin's aggression, petitioners' pigs, and the Peeps' involvement with his daughter that he hadn't slept well lately. "Thank you for sharing the pipe." He released his long toke into the den. "My Uncle, are you still connected to the shaman community in other tribes?"

"Unh." Mohiinok exhaled again and coughed.

"Good. I'd like to ask you for a favor. It concerns my daughter. I'm not sure you remember, but you met her once and gave her a tribal pendant. She's always treasured it. Well, she's a teenager now. Her mother left us, and I can't seem to…" The President's voice broke. For unknown reasons he felt vulnerable around this old man. The shaman did not utter any judgments of his parenting, but perhaps his own guilt was playing ventriloquist. Peabody regained his composure and continued. "…I can't seem to get through to her at all." The President of the world's greatest national power humbly waited for the go-ahead from the world's tiniest wrinkled Algonquian shaman.

"What does your spirit want from my spirit, Nephew?"

"Sarantha has become involved with a small group of people who want to drastically change the government. They believe they can do it without violence. They call themselves the Peeps." He paused and took another toke. "I'd like to give her some leeway with them; maybe it will inspire her to go into politics. Maybe it will…" His voice trailed off and for thirty seconds, all was quiet. Peabody felt some part of his forebrain – call it the gate attendant --duck through a turnstile and run away. " Uh, sorry. Lost my train of thought."

Mohiinok gazed into Peabody's face. "You look so white. Good thing. If you can't think better than that when you smoke the pipe, Nephew, at least you won't bring shame to the Algonquian." Suddenly the shaman's eyes twinkled. "Make Jello!"

"Uncle, did you just ask for Jello?"

"Unh. Doesn't Jello sound good?" The elderly man grinned. He still had most of his teeth, although he wouldn't appear in any whitening commercials.

Peabody thought about it and decided Jello did sound good. He pulled out his cell, texted the Camp David kitchen supervisor and ordered two bowls of the jiggly dessert.

"Unh?" the elder gestured at Peabody's cell phone.

The President nodded. "Job requirement. Do you have a cell phone, Uncle? When I invited you here, I reached you through your reservation's admin office."

The shaman considered the cell phone like it was a shiny turd and shook his head. "Have other ways of hearing, knowing."

When the Jello arrived, Peabody brought in the bowls of squiggly dark maroon rectangles, napkins and spoons, placed the offerings before Mohiinok, and closed the den door again to assure their privacy. The shaman took a big spoonful, and swished the Jello around in his mouth for a moment.

"Helps with dry mouth," he declared after he swallowed.

Peabody stared at the dessert bowl. A wave of silliness and dry mouth overcame him. He thrust both hands into his bowl and squished the Jello through his fingers with the delight of a two-year-old finger painting. Finally the munchies passed. He ate the remaining dessert with a spoon and used his napkin to wipe both face and fingers clean. With careful effort he gathered his thoughts once more and began his request. "Here's what I thought, Uncle. If I assign the FBI or Secret Service to follow these Peeps, the whole situation will either leak to the public, or this Peeps group will realize they're being followed by the government, and will dump Sarantha. You understand?"

The shaman finished the pipe. More coughing wracked his chest. Suddenly he looked out the window at the exact moment about fifty birds flew from one of the trees surrounding the building. Mohiinok chuckled and turned to Peabody. "Did you sense the fox spirit? Fox will have to find herself another dinner tonight."

Peabody looked out the window at the scattering birds. How the hell had Mohiinok noticed a fox outdoors while sitting on the floor looking out the window? How did he know the exact instant the birds would take flight? Was there some symbolic message in the shaman's mention of birds? He tried again. "Uncle, I need to know if you'll help me in this situation with my daughter. These people she's associating with – these Peeps – they live all over the country. If you still have a connections with other tribes, we could use their help to keep an eye on these folks, and report if there's any danger to Sarantha."

"Unh." That was all Mohiinok said for a long minute, then he recited a lengthy meandering Algonquian folk tale about a woman who turned men into fish.

Peabody was so stoned it was hard to figure out how to get an answer. After letting his mind float for another few minutes, he tethered his frontal cortex and tried again. "Uncle, please, can you help me with this? Will you communicate with other shamans around the country and ask them to send people to keep an eye on these Peeps rebels, to protect my daughter?"

"If a woman can turn men into fish, we can protect your beautiful daughter as she grows into a full human being."

After the weekend at Camp David, Mohiinok returned to his village. He contacted shamans and tribal councils in every area where the Peeps resided. Kickapoo, Mojave, Ute, Coushatta, Sac and Fox, Paiute and Shoshone would appoint strong, discreet adults who could stealthily track without drawing attention to themselves. As Peabody well knew from his childhood exposure to tribal folks, no one could disappear better than an Indian who didn't want to be noticed. These 'agents' would track the Peeps' daily activities, alert Mohiinok if Sarantha showed up at any of their locations, and report any danger.

President Peabody's unofficial spy network was in place.

It wasn't until he'd returned to the White House Sunday night that he grew curious about something. He phoned Mohiinok at the reservation. "Uncle, if you still have such powerful connections with so many tribes, I wondered – did the Algonquians in Pennsylvania know you were at Camp David?"

The President heard the shaman chuckle. "Who you think really scared them birds outta the trees?"

Chapter 15

Like neon Peeps candies self-propelling across a chess board, trailing sugar crystals and covert intent, the team continued their revolutionary efforts.

Los Angeles, CA: Raven agreed to publicize the need for a SuperGrid which everyone knew would take decades to build if they had to abide by current environmental regulations. She tapped a few favors within her world of TV media and wrangled herself an appearance on a top morning news show to push their cause. She felt this was contribution enough on her part, considering her respect for environmental concerns, and the fact that her fiancé would be home on leave for the holidays. So much to do! Prep for the morning show, early holiday shopping, bikini wax...

San Diego, CA: Navya and her husband were Range Rovering through potholes of doubt and briars of boredom in their marriage. Navya had exceeded real estate sales goals. She'd traveled the world. Her children were grown and doing well. Her husband, an ENT specialist, buried himself in his work. It did not help Navya to know she was less interesting than an ear canal or deviated septum. Something long suppressed was rising up from her marrow, thirsting for creative expression. She quilted once in a while, but didn't knit or crochet. When she baked it was by recipe, without intuition. She didn't paint, sculpt or draw. But she was extremely good at selling commercial real estate. She was persuasive and she knew it. She was sure she could put that persuasion to work for the Peeps.

In between an elevator ride at Boldwell Cankor, the nail salon, and a chocolate truffle, Navya experienced her first creative brainstorm. She convinced herself that her powers of persuasion were more than adequate to make a social media video advocating for Make Regs Make Sense. She would direct a video-- an unusual, provocative and memorable video! She would have an American hero explain, in a dramatic fashion, why the country needed the Make Regs Make Sense bill. She shared few specifics with her fellow Peeps, preferring her contribution to be a surprise. Since Navya was a successful business woman who supported the bill, the group trusted that whatever she had up her sari would be fine.

Sheridan, OR: Emery was writing what he hoped would be a meaningful Thanksgiving sermon. He'd increased public relations efforts to create prison/community interactions, one of which was a Christmas play performed by the inmates. This time Mean Larry chose to play Joseph. Emery bought holiday gifts for his parents and siblings, and prayed for peace. But more than any other activity during the holiday season, Emery devoted time and effort into arranging romantic encounters with his new lover, Matt Sandstone. Sometimes Matt would drive down to Sheridan, near Portland. Sometimes Emery could manage the time off to visit Matt in Seattle. Wherever they connected, they left empty condom wrappers on the night stands and love notes under the pillows. But Emery let the Peeps know that, as busy as he was, if they needed him for something specific with the Make Regs Make Sense bill, he was willing to help.

Dallas, TX: Vivi would spend her holiday break with her new friend Einar. At last she'd see if his eyes were that green in real life and not just online. Her parents felt hurt and concerned, but with Borgs and with teenagers, resistance is futile. Knowing Vivi's heart was already halfway to Iceland, Glenda asked if she could contribute anything to the Make Regs effort. Vivi replied, *"Between now and Christmas, I'll cover your asses regarding online security, but that's all I have time for. ¿Comprendes?"*

New Orleans, LA: The holidays are a busy time for restaurants and DeVille's was no exception. When he wasn't comparing produce prices or researching the perfect rice grain, he was fu jingle-mingle-tingling from stress, confusing customers when Jingle Bells played on the sound system.

St. Louis, MO: Glenda checked her Match profile, hoping for a date on New Year's Eve. Finding only a message from an admittedly alcoholic 28-year-old in the Ukraine, she switched gears and brainstormed a Plan B in case the Peeps' efforts failed. She was pretty sure they would. When her Havanese jumped on her lap and angled for attention, she scratched behind his ears. "It's not that I'm a pessimist," she clarified to Socrates, "it's just that I know my history."

Boulder, CO: All of the Peeps agreed that the key role in raising the nation's awareness of the need for common sense regulation would fall on Ted's shoulders. After all, Make Regs Make Sense was his baby. And he'd come up with one hell of a plan.

Raven fussed with a wayward strand of hair. She wasn't fond of what the stylist for the "Java Jake" show had arranged. She was cued in during a commercial break. She settled herself and checked her earpiece while viewers watched a toothpaste commercial. Her hosts Jake Farberra and Nikki Spryzenski, Republican and Democrat respectively, were relaxed and friendly.

"You're executive producer of the new TV show, Power Up!, an American Idol type competition for green energy projects," Nikki began. "The young man who invented Fricking first appeared on your show."

"You could say he gave us a Fricking good start!" Raven joked.

Nikki gave a meaningful look at Java Jake who took the baton. "We understand there's only so much benefit Fricking can bring to the energy scene, though," Jake Farberra said. "What's going on? What's the problem?"

"Simply put," Raven began, "we now have more green electricity than we can safely handle on our existing power grid. America desperately needs a true SuperGrid. Several, in fact."

"We've needed a great deal of modernized infrastructure for years, but Congress seems incapable of making it happen. The EPA regulations alone can delay a project for ye…"

Nikki interrupted Joe. "What good is having plenty of energy if the air you breathe or the water you drink is toxic?"

Raven joined in. "All I know is that it's a shame to have affordable green energy available and not be able to use it. Americans are a sensible people; maybe we can come up with sensible solutions. There's a deregulation bill in Congress that could help speed up construction of a SuperGrid."

Jake Farberra replied, "How refreshing to hear someone who supports green energy also supports deregulation."

With uncharacteristic snip, Nikki announced, "We'll be back with the latest update on Malaysian Airlines flight 370 right after this message."

Ted played with his girlfriend's auburn curls as she drove him to the Denver airport. "You've sure had a lot of energy lately!" she said, smiling. What an understatement! She'd be walking funny for a week. Never a slouch in bed, Ted had been up for extra innings last night.

"I'm in the zone, babe. I'm off to do something that will make a difference. I feel shit-kickin' good."

"What's this secret mission of yours, sweetie? What are you up to?"

"I already told you– it's a secret. I can't say much; other people are involved. If it were just me…" Ted glanced at her pouting lower lip and smiled. "Besides, if I pull this off, you won't have to hear about it from me. You'll see it on the news. Now get me to the airport before I miss my flight!"

Ted landed at Newark airport at 5:43 pm on a crisp early November evening. The time difference between Colorado and the east coast played to his advantage. He wanted to do this at night when there would be less air traffic, particularly those pesky tourist helicopters.

He took a shuttle to the private aircraft hanger and rented a Cessna 150. It was a saucy little number not more than three years old. In all of his flight lessons, he hadn't piloted a plane this well equipped; the student trainers he was used to were junk heaps by comparison.

From his baggage Ted retrieved a large reel threaded with 600 feet of plastic ribbon. He ran his fingers over the mechanism, verifying that the ribbon flowed smoothly over the reel, then locked the reel and secured it to the Cessna's wing strut. He slipped the release cable through the Cessna's cockpit window, got inside, and taxied out for take-off.

On the runway he informed the control tower that he'd be flying VFR, Visual Flight Rules--no flight plan needed or expected. They gave him clearance for Take Off and the sweet little Cessna soared into the evening sky.

Ted's heart soared, too, as he headed north to NY via Sandy Hook toward the Hudson River. He was a naturally gifted pilot, and like most of us, he loved doing what he was good at. He'd never felt more fully alive than he did at this moment. He'd soon enter restricted air space, the East River Exclusion Special Flight Rules Area. At the elevation he required, the FAA might easily assess him as a terrorist and authorize shooting him down. His strategy required playing dumb and flying smart.

At 1500 feet, he gazed at the bustling Big Apple below. So many people, so many lives. So many lights. So many buildings. So much bureaucracy. So many regulations. Make Regs Make Sense was needed, was important. But was it worth risking his life for?

When Ted was certain he'd entered restricted air space, he radioed in. "LaGuardia Tower? This is Cessna November3469Foxtrot." The tower must've been busy because not only did he not see any military jets ready to play Terminal Velocity, he didn't even get a response. He repeated the message three times before the tower blasted back.

"November3469Foxtrot, this is LaGuardia Tower."

"LaGuardia Tower, November3469Foxtrot." Ted tried to sound scared. Knowing he could be blasted out of the universe any second enhanced his acting skills. "I'm a solo student and I'm lost."

The air traffic controller at LaGuardia responded. "November3469Foxtrot, squawk 1819 and Ident." As Ted had expected, the tower was asking him to push the Cessna's transponder allowing the tower to identify him on their radar screens. He needed to reassure them but he also needed to buy himself time. He reduced his altitude and moved closer to his target. He then entered "1891" and pushed the transponder, knowing the tower would remain unable to track him.

Soon she was less than a quarter mile in front of him, a woman of perfect carriage, standing on a star-like platform wearing a long flowing gown: Lady Liberty! "Come to me, Baby!"

LaGuardia belched at him again about identifying for the control tower. When he reached 1000' elevation, he entered 1819 on the transponder, giving LaGuardia eyes on him at last. That might stave off missiles another minute or two.

The tower responded heatedly, "November 3469Foxtrot, you're in restricted air space! What's your destination?"

Ted depressed the output button on his mike. "69 Foxtrot. I'm working on my cross country and got disoriented. My destination's..." Ted popped a stick of beef jerky in his mouth, chomped on it twice, and finished his communication, "*yefrigden.*"

"69Foxtrot, we didn't copy. Repeat: What's your destination?" The nervous controller's adrenaline level was spiking.

So was Ted's. He answered, again enunciating through the jerky. "69 Foxtrot, I'm *pshewtunt* and low on fuel."

"69Foxtrot, what's your destination?" The poor controller was about to stroke out.

Ted spotted an Air National Guard jet on his port side. "69Foxtrot, my destination is Linden, sir."

"69Foxtrot, turn left, heading two seven zero, immediately!"

Ted smiled to himself. Yeah, you and the horse you rode in on. Ted continued to tease the control tower with muffled responses, half-assed questions and inappropriate responses – all non-threatening – while he approached Liberty Island. They'd figured out his agenda soon enough, but if he was skilled, he'd have just enough time to accomplish his mission.

He descended another few hundred feet and positioned himself directly over the great Lady's head. He pulled the release cable on the reel of plastic ribbon, heard it unsnap, and watched the ribbon unroll and dangle. After only two tries, the red ribbon caught on one of the spikes of Lady Liberty's corona. Ted was soaring on lift --not just the aerodynamic kind. His spirits were higher than the F-16s deployed to spot him. He felt unable to tame the smile on his face. Life should be filled with moments like these!

Soon red plastic ribbon draped the Statue's arm, chin and body. Every circle he flew around the statue represented greater and greater risk. The only tourist helicopter operating at this hour approached him, pissing Ted off and skewing his natural piloting ability for a few seconds. But he recovered and continued to drape the *grande dame*, until the symbol of America was bound in red tape.

Now every second counted. When he heard the reel snap with the last of the plastic ribbon, he tossed out a box of pamphlets Glenda had written about the dangers of over-regulation.

He picked up his mike and radioed, "LaGuardia, 3469Foxtrot will adjust course." By the next morning, most of America knew 3469Foxtrot was not a lost flight student. Both traditional and social media gave him more coverage than he could have hoped for, and with every opportunity, Ted explained the virtues of fewer government regulations. He delighted in pointing out that it was both legal and illegal to fly around the Statue of Liberty, depending on whether you flew clockwise or counterclockwise. The FAA had its own regs mess. Within 48 hours, he was released on his own recognizance. After all, he'd only flown counterclockwise.

Navya contacted Raven via their online chat room. Navya: Raven, I need an actor who can play Martin Luther King. Can you help?

Raven: What does MLK have to do with Make Regs Make Sense?

Navya: I have an idea based on one of his famous speeches.

Raven: I don't get the connection, but let me think...how about David Oyelowo? He played King in *Selma*.

Navya: No, I think he might be too recognizable for my purposes. Anyone else come to mind?

Raven thought for a moment, then typed: An actor named Dennis Tines could use the work. He's a decent guy, and he's been delivering pizzas long enough to appreciate any kind of acting gig that pays.

Navya: This pays. I'll drive to L.A. next Wednesday with a script and videographer.

Raven: I'll let Dennis know. Maybe we can do lunch while you're in town.

The social media-sphere covered every possible opinion, fact, foible and photo of Ted's Statue of Liberty bondage act. A percentage of citizens even wrote Congress and pushed for Cannon's Make Regs Make Sense bill, which passed the House and was sent to the Senate. By that time, consumers of social media had moved on to speculative posts about whether President Peabody had hair plugs -- until they saw a particular new You Tube video. The source of the video remained untraceable, although the poster had used the pseudonym MumbaiBabe113.

A somber-looking African American man with a fair resemblance to Martin Luther King, Jr. addressed the viewer from what looked like the Washington Mall, although the video sent subliminal clues that the setting was a graphic simulation. The video was shot in black and white and a filter had been used to make it appear grainy. The actor mimicked the cadence and intonation of Martin Luther King, Jr. beautifully.

"In the Bible, the book of Amos, chapter 5, verse 24, Almighty God told the children of Israel, 'Let justice roll down like waters, and righteousness like an ever-flowing stream.' Let me say that again. 'Let justice roll down like waters, and righteousness like an ever-flowing stream.' The Almighty did *not* say, 'Let legalism roll down like waters and regulations like an over-flowing sewer drain.' No, indeed, brothers and sisters. No, indeed. The Almighty does not want legalism and regulations to smother your just impulses! Legalism is not justice, brothers and sisters! Do I hear an Amen? Legalism is not justice. Legalism offers rules without context, without common sense, without compassion."

The clip ended with a close-up of the actor gazing into the distance. Superimposed over his face was bright yellow text that urged: Tell Congress to vote Yes on the Make Regulation Make Sense bill!

A handsome young guy circling Lady Liberty had flare, but using one of Martin Luther King, Jr.'s speeches to push a traditionally conservative issue lacked political savvy. As Glenda watched the video, she cringed. She instructed Vivi to delete it from You Tube, while simultaneously smoothing her eyebrows as if life itself depended on them. She phoned Navya. "What were you thinking, woman?"

Navya had followed the hundreds of indignant, angry, even threatening comments posted in response to the video and knew she'd screwed up. "I was familiar with King's "Let Justice roll down like waters" speech and, you know, I thought it would make a great contrast –justice versus legalism."

"Did you run this little idea of yours by any other Peep? Did anyone agree that it was cool to use an African-American hero for this purpose?"

"I'm a woman of color, aren't I?" Navya asked defensively.

"Yes, you are a woman of color. From Mumbai. Who's wealthy. Who's a Republican. You didn't exactly march with Martin Luther King. From now on, none of the Peeps launches any effort unless everyone of us is on board."

The Daily Show's Trevor Noah had a field day with the video. Governor Nikki Haley commented in an editorial that women from India were women of color, too, and had a right to express their opinions.

Oprah's social media team tweeted: Would this MumbaiBabe113 like to see an actor who resembled Gandhi push adult diapers?

Ouch.

By the time Whoopi Goldberg, Ann Coulter and Supriya Jindal weighed in, the Make Regs Make Sense bill was toxic for Democrats – and Democrats controlled the Senate.

###

Bayne Stane's butt rested on the padded oval seat. The royal blue porcelain and tile surrounding him reflected a pristine shine he failed to appreciate. The founder and CEO of a multinational telecommunication and satellite corporation glanced down past his hairless legs to the rumpled slacks at his feet, and focused on the phone conversation he was having with conservative radio talk show icon Nate Festring.

"I'm not sure I follow you, Mr. Stane," said Festring. He puffed his cigar, buying himself time and edging himself closer to an inevitable stroke. Festring was a professional communicator, but he had a difficult time relating to Bayne Stane. The man shaved all of his body hair. The only color he wore was gray. He didn't believe in evolution and thought cursive handwriting prideful. He'd commissioned a sculpture made from longhorn skulls, Studebaker grills, and recovered pieces of SkyLab, on top of which he mounted a flat surface, creating what looked like an altar. He installed it in the center of his living room. Once when Festring had attended a fundraiser at Stane's home, he'd half expected Abraham to emerge from a guest room and sacrifice Isaac on the damned thing.

A devout Roman Catholic, Stane had been brought into the Republican fold via a Tea Party SuperPac several years ago. He'd remained a staunch and generous GOP supporter, but now he was using his money and back channels to block the Senate from introducing the best regulations bill Congress had ever seen.

Festring really wished his pal Senator Lacomb hadn't asked him to probe Stane on the issue. The radio show host continued. "This new bill will streamline regulations and stimulate the economy. I know you're a solid conservative. What's your hesitation, if I may ask?"

Bayne Stane allowed peristalsis to do its work while he answered Festring. "I support Cannon's regs bill. But the anti-abortion bill needs to be the number one priority. I've given the party money for years; you know I have. I supported the GOP even when it looked like that heathen Hrump would get the nod. But frankly I'm tired of hearing how, as soon as we pass this, or as soon as we pass that, Congress will outlaw abortion. I cannot in good conscience allow this travesty to continue. I want action." Stane flushed and moved to the bidet.

"Is that water I hear in the background?" Festring asked.

"Having a new filtration system installed." He washed and dried his hands. "Look, Nate – you have a great show; you've made your mark in the world. But imagine for one moment: what if the next Nate Festring enters this world as a tiny fetus whose mom doesn't want him? Don't you think that's just as important as picking up a sickle and clearing the regulations thicket?"

Did Stane just mention fetuses and sickles in the same sentence? Festring sighed. "I see your point, Mr. Stane. I'll talk to some people; see what I can do."

"You'll address the need for anti-abortion legislation on air?"

"Of course, of course. I..."

"Excellent." There was a soft scratching in the background, then silence.

"Are you still there, Mr. Stane?"

"I just wrote a check with a lot of zeroes in it – a donation to the Nate Festring Museum of Radio Broadcasting."

"Well, thank you, Mr. Stane." Festring shifted in his chair, uncomfortable at the level of kiss-ass required of him.

"Don't thank me yet. I'll mail the check the day the President signs a meaningful anti-abortion bill into law."

Festring visualized many dollars swirling down a drain, an image Bayne Stane might have found surprisingly apt.

###

Glenda put down the laundry she was folding and picked up the call on the second ring. She activated the new security software on her cell Vivi had instructed them to use. "Hello, Navya. What's up?" Seeing Navya's name on Incoming Call was not exactly reassuring to Glenda at this juncture.

"I called Representative Cannon today to get an update on the progress of the regs bill. The Democrats won't budge; the Senate Majority Leader won't bring it to the floor."

"Well, we may have to let things cool down a while."

"I know I screwed up with the video, but it was an honest mistake and I..." Navya's voice trailed off.

Glenda let her dangle there a while, then asked, "Did Cannon suggest any strategies?"

Navya sighed with frustration. "Cannon's as stymied as we are. He said the Senate Majority Leader won't introduce our regs bill unless they exempt the EPA, just like you suspected might happen. And some mega-donor behind the scenes wants an anti-abortion bill passed before the regs bill can even be introduced. Then there's Peabody. The President won't support the regs bill until Senator Lacomb endorses his tax reform proposal. Why should regulation reform be held hostage by abortion or tax reform? Oh, and a junior Senator from Kansas wants to require a certain number of community service volunteer hours before citizens could serve on the committees that review regulations."

"Well, that doesn't sound so terrible," Glenda responded. "We'll have to compromise in at least a few ways if we're going to get this bill passed into law."

"Yes, but the Kansas Senator wants the community service hours to be performed at local churches."

"Oh." An unapologetic atheist, Glenda understood the problems inherent in that.

Navya continued. "I've been trying to track the intricacies of who's doing what to whom, and for what favors and trade-offs, but Congress is more byzantine than the business moguls I deal with! I binged-watched 15 episodes of West Wing and..."

"You did what?" Glenda inquired with disbelief.

"I watched West Wing, you know, to try to understand the machinations of Congress. I thought of it as a tutorial. Didn't help much; I'm still confused!" She paused and popped another Xocolatl de David salted caramel into her mouth. More subdued, she asked, "Is this it, Glenda? Do we give up?"

Glenda tossed three damp towels back into the dryer. "Remember when we all first met at Logan Airport, and we set out on this venture? We did so because we all realized government doesn't work well for the American people any more. I thought it best to try legitimate methods first, but I have a Plan B."

Glenda called a meeting of the Peeps in their online chat room.

Glenda: Hello, everyone. I have an alternative plan for how to get the regs bill through the Senate, but... it's risky and may not work. I'm open to suggestions if someone comes up with a better idea.

No better ideas appeared on the chat room screen, so Glenda continued typing.

Glenda: There's a Democrat Senator from North Dakota who's about to retire, Senator Roscoe Anders. He's working on a piece of legislation called the Road Kill Bill.

Vivi's rapidly typed response appeared on the screen. Vivi: Kill Bill, like the movie? Road Kill Bill? GTFO!

Glenda ignored the interruption. Glenda: His State Highway Department's been in a budget crunch for a while, and apparently road kill can be a real problem up near the Canadian border. His Road Kill Bill would allow states to use National Guard equipment like bulldozers, trucks and wheel loaders to remove animal carcasses. Dead caribou can block a country road for days. And by the time they locate equipment to remove it, the smell is horrible.

Navya: Dead caribou--seriously?

Glenda: Yes, seriously. And probably an occasional moose or bear. Right now the National Guard won't let them use the equipment because the head of North Dakota's National Guard thinks it's unclear whether Guard equipment paid for by <u>federal</u> tax dollars can be used for work on <u>state</u> highways.

Emery: But the equipment's just sitting in some National Guard depot, right? Seems silly that it couldn't be used to clean up a state highway.

Ted: Silly? Try stupid—that's big government at work!

Vivi: So what's our plan?

Glenda: This Road Kill Bill is what we need – no one is going to read it through, start to finish, except possibly Senator Anders. No one else cares. If we can convince the Senator that inserting our regs bill into his Road Kill Bill is an honorable thing for the country, he may go for it. He's about to retire; he can take greater risks than a younger or more prominent Senator.

Clearly Glenda was the strategist among them.

Ted: How do we get the Senator to agree to this?

Glenda: Emery, how would you like to be the first gay James Bond?

Chapter 16

Senator Roscoe Anders, a pale 68-year-old ignoring early Parkinson's tremors in his left hand, studied the man seated across from him in his office in Bismarck. Navy blue two-button worsted wool suit. Crisp white shirt. Bacco Bucci leather shoes. A modest Timex. Good posture. Silver streaked the fellow's thick black hair. The agent looked 40-ish, was swarthy and had a 5 o'clock shadow at 1 P.M. They must be recruiting people who look Middle Eastern, Anders thought, someone who can infiltrate a terrorist cell. Senator Anders sensed something else about this fellow, too, but what? He seemed to lack the edginess or arrogance Anders associated with intelligence agents. Yet a secretary from the Defense Intelligence Agency had arranged this meeting, and the man's badge and credentials looked fine.

Emery, who'd presented a damned good replica of a DIA badge identifying him as Agent Mark Kairos, waited patiently, examining the worn arms of the Senator's leather chair, the musty bookshelves, the hurricane lantern desk lamps and the moose head mounted on the wall.

In Senator Anders' estimation, intelligence agencies were among the most miserable performers in government. He'd spent four years on the Senate Intelligence Committee. By the time he'd managed to extricate himself from the committee, he'd decided national intelligence was an oxymoron. Intelligence agencies suspected hundreds of plots that never existed. They ignored dangerous behavioral patterns that should have been obvious. They raked taxpayers for millions and tucked the funds into shadow accounts. They were turf-worshippers. They threatened innocent Americans. When they detained someone, you never knew if that person would disappear forever or if they'd play by the rules and bend over backwards trying to be politically correct. There were over 1270 government organizations working on intelligence, counterterrorism, and homeland security, yet Senator Anders was fairly sure you could learn as much about security threats by reading tea leaves or Tweets. And yet, and yet…. When Al Quaeda targeted the Twin Towers, when ISIS made Paris explode, when Sabad poisoned the Milan water supply… "How can I help you, Agent Kairos?"

"Senator," Emery began, "This conversation must remain absolutely confidential. The U.S. government needs your help, and we need our exchange to be off the record. As in, it never happened. You understand?"

The Senator's head, situated below and slightly to the right of the moose head, bobbed up and down in affirmation.

Emery continued. "Perhaps the DIA's greatest challenge is to identify and defend against *any* and *all* threats to our national security. We can't afford to only look at threats from terrorists. Or traitors. Or WikiLeaks. We need to look at the big picture to ensure America remains a strong, vibrant nation." Emery modulated his voice to use the empathetic, persuasive tone he employed in pastoral counseling. "Frankly, we're up against it, Senator. We have identified a serious national security threat…" Here Emery added drama to his tone, *"from within our own government."*

Startled, Senator Anders leaned forward and whispered. "Are you suggesting you know of government officials planning to commit treasonous acts?"

Emery met the Senator's intensity. He continued, speaking without a hint of humor. "Have you traveled to Singapore, Senator?"

The Senator shook his head No, and Emery continued. "Or Barcelona? Shanghai? Sydney? The rest of the world is putting America to shame. Our roads and transportation systems are a joke. We can't build a SuperGrid for the new green electricity available through Fricking. Many of our bridges should require drivers to sign a consent form before they drive over them. Right here in North Dakota, you can't use National Guard equipment to clear roads. It borders on insanity. Soon no one wants to visit the Grand Canyon or open a new office building in Atlanta. If we cannot dramatically improve our infrastructure, Senator, the U.S. will continue to lose commercial and tourism dollars. According to DIA's predictive models software, over-regulation will force the U.S. into second-tier nation status by 2020."

Senator Anders now pushed back in his chair and looked at Emery silently for several long moments, putting the conversational ball in Emery's court.

Emery continued. "A new bill on regulatory reform made its way through the House recently--perhaps you've heard of it--the Cannon Make Regulation Make Sense bill?"

Senator Anders felt his pulse quicken. "That's the bill being pushed by that terrible Martin Luther King, Jr. video, right?"

Why couldn't he have instead remembered the valiant pilot who draped the Statue of Liberty in red tape, thought Emery, as he brainstormed a response. "An unfortunate truth, and we're investigating that. Nevertheless, the bill itself is badly needed, Senator. Our country simply cannot remain a world economic leader much longer. And if we can't remain an economic leader, we won't remain a military leader."

"And exactly how does the intelligence community imagine that one almost-retired North Dakota Senator can help?"

"We'd like you to insert the text of the regulation reform bill into your Road Kill Bill as an amendment. For the good of your country."

Senator Anders laughed out loud. "You can't be serious! Why, any meaningful regulations bill will be at least several hundred pages long. No way the clerks who prepare the bill aren't going to notice an amendment that size!"

Emery was thankful the Peeps had anticipated this. "We've created a much shorter version of the bill. We tightened language, deleted repetitions, and hyperlinked external references. We've crunched it down to 18 pages."

"Eighteen pages, eh?" Anders thought for a moment. "What if I agree; what if we insert your 18-page abbreviated regs bill into the Road Kill Bill. Then what? Aren't you worried that media folks assigned to Congress will leak news that the bill contains an unexpected amendment?"

"The DIA will provide …" Emery chose his words carefully, "certain distractions, if you will, to keep the news media otherwise occupied. If your Road Kill Bill doesn't get much scrutiny, we believe it will pass into law. North Dakota will get the road kill removal equipment it needs and America will begin a reasonable deregulation process that will allow infrastructure renewal."

Senator Anders leaned back in his chair. The reasons Agent Kairos had given him were a crock of caca; he was pretty certain of that. He figured the truth lay closer to Republican lobbyists exerting pressure on a mid-level DIA manager who had an interest in deregulation. Anders knew the Senate Majority Leader Frank Winston had refused to introduce the regulations bill for fear the EPA would be gutted. Anders wasn't sure who or what was behind this request, or why the intelligence community was involved in the matter. But he knew he'd retire in January. He knew he'd never particularly liked Frank Winston. He knew many voters back home thought the EPA went overboard. He knew it was an arbitrary power trip by the National Guard when they'd told him they weren't sure their equipment could be used for state v. federal purposes. And he knew folks back home sure as hell wanted dead caribou removed from their roads. What the hell, he figured. Why not? He leaned forward, matching his body language to Emery's. "It's a deal, Agent Kairos. After all, I wouldn't want to turn down an opportunity to make America more secure now, would I?"

After departing Senator Anders' office, Emery walked half a block before he sensed someone following him. He turned quickly and caught a glimpse of a dark haired, dark eyed person who appeared Native American. Hmm, thought Emery. That's a little weird, but there are several reservations in North Dakota.

###

The following week the Peeps kicked into full gear with plans for media distraction. Navya was forgiven; new assignments were issued via their secure chat room.

For the first distraction, Raven recruited an L.A. plumber/wannabe actor with a noticeable facial resemblance to Lady Gaga. The actor was told to give an interview on camera, acting as though he were, indeed, Lady Gaga and that s/he had decided s/he was transgender. From now on, the eager media were told, there was no Lady Gaga, only Lord Gaga.

Eight minutes after the video was posted on social media, the real Lady Gaga returned fire. Social media exchanges lobbed back and forth. Vivi and her benevolent-hacker pal Einar securely hid the origin of the Lord Gaga posts. At first Lady Gaga threatened law suits, but when no one could determine who was behind the Lord Gaga rumors, she good-naturedly used the spotlight to support transgender issues.

The distraction only worked for three days, but during that time, not one dot of ink appeared in any major newspaper or social media outlet about the Road Kill Bill. Even the political elite had gone Gaga.

Glenda then spent an afternoon at the St. Louis Public Library, skimming professional science magazines and taking notes. She returned home and prepared a press release.

University of Astuce
Provost Office
Building 12
1200 Rue de Royale
Montreal, Canada
PRESS RELEASE
For Immediate Release
Contact: Vincent Gabriel, Media Relations
Phone: 800.463.3339
Email: vgabriel@media.univastuce.edu

The University of Astuce in Montreal has announced the discovery in seismology of a phenomenon known as 'mute earthquakes.' Professor Fan Li-Chin, who holds a Ph.D. in Geophysics, recently detected a mute earthquake at the University of Astuce's seismology lab and was able to replicate the phenomenon. Mute earthquakes are miniscule tremors in the earth's mantle, so deep below the earth's surface that, although their presence had been theorized, they had never before been detected. The significance of mute earthquakes is still being debated by the scientific community. Dr. Fan theorizes they are precursors of regular earthquakes and could possibly be used in alert systems once the techniques have been refined. Dr. Fan will demonstrate his mute earthquake detection technique at the Seismology and Cosmology Symposium this April.

The media ran the story, pulling energy and focus away from Congressional matters. A San Francisco Chronicle reporter contacted FEMA to ask if they would begin utilizing mute earthquakes as part of the Earthquake and Tsunami Emergency Alert System. A few hours later FEDEX called the San Francisco Chronicle, complaining that FEDEX's Montreal phone number had appeared erroneously in an article about mute earthquakes. The phone calls irritated them and interfered with business. It took FEDEX's protest to motivate reporters to delve into the matter. Glenda had hoped the press release would distract for several days, but she'd settle for a day and a half.

That week Prince William, Kate Middleton (the Duchess of Cambridge), and the royal youngsters were scheduled to visit New York City. While the event itself provided some media distraction, the Peeps decided to enhance it. Glenda wrote an email purportedly from the Chief of the NYPD's elite Mounted Unit; Vivi insured the origin of the email could not be traced. The email instructed all NYPD equine police, at the moment the royal family arrived at LaGuardia, to charge through the streets on horseback wearing rented revolutionary war costumes, waving their guns in the air, yelling, "The British are coming! The British are coming!" The email explained it was an approved public relations event, with the full blessing of the mayor and the royals.

It takes something remarkable to catch the average New York pedestrian's attention. Horses galloping full speed through traffic shouting "The British are coming!" did the trick. When citizens began calling the mayor's office to ask about the event or to complain of traffic issues caused by the Revere-esque ride, the mayor's office was caught off guard. They did not want to appear to have dropped the ball on a major PR event, so they defaulted to 'of course we knew about this.' Before the day ended, workers were sweeping road apples from in front of the Museum of Natural History and the Duchess of Cambridge was telling reporters how much her young children enjoyed the equestrian antics. A Staten Island movie theater capitalized on the stunt by initiating a special tribute to "The Russians Are Coming! The Russians Are Coming!" God bless American enterprise. The rider ruckus provided new directions for the media spotlight -- for two days, anyway.

Meanwhile, Senator Anders had added the 18-page condensed version of the Make Regs Make Sense bill as an amendment to his Road Kill Bill and was pushing it through the Senate. Nobody – not other senators, not lobbyists, and certainly not the media who were experiencing the unusual problem of too many things to cover – cared. To be fair, Senator Anders did care, and he was pretty sure that any of his constituents who'd ever had a rotting caribou carcass on one of their roads cared, too. For the Road Kill Bill, it was "so far, so good." The Peeps were encouraged.

Raven had come up with an idea, a rumor to be leaked on social media. She intimated that the information had come from a reliable inside source, something she, as an ex-reporter, knew how to do. She leaked that Vice President Athena Storm had a tattoo of a rhino on her butt. For whatever reasons, the story had legs. People tweeted, posted on Facebook, and talked around the office water cooler, speculating whether the tattoo was of a real rhinoceros or merely a fancy inscription of the word RINO. Social media rumors persisted until Vice President Storm, a woman of uncommon common sense, held a press conference and asked what possible difference it made in the lives of Americans what she might have tattooed on her gluteus. With pragmatism and humor, she communicated her belief that it was far more important that she didn't just sit on her gluteus – tattooed or otherwise – but that she worked for the American people.

It's the duty of the Office of the Executive Clerk to deliver approved bills to the White House for the President to sign into law. Simon Berry, the Executive Clerk, received an invitation to a holiday party at the home of Bayne Stane, the eccentric satellite communications mogul. While Stane often courted senators and political insiders, Simon Berry was surprised he'd personally been included on the guest list.

He and his wife attended the gala, grazing on persimmon bruschetta canapés, sipping Bollinger Les Vieilles Vignes Francaises cuvée, hobnobbing with the Gingriches, the Bushes, the Ryans, and other power players, most of them Roman Catholic. For the sake of their appetites and spirits, Berry and his wife tried to avoid the ugly-ass sculpture Stane had installed in his living room.

They'd been there about forty minutes when Stane himself approached, dressed in a dove gray shirt and charcoal gray suit and tie. "Might I speak to you privately for a few minutes?" Stane asked Berry. "I'm sure your lovely wife will do fine mingling with the other guests for a while." Without waiting for an answer, Stane took Berry by the elbow and escorted him to a private back office.

They sat in overstuffed chairs near a fireplace. Berry felt wary; word around the Beltway was that Stane had almost as many neuroses as Howard Hughes. He felt tension in his shoulders as Stane leaned toward him in conversation. "Simon – may I call you Simon?"

A nod from Berry.

"Simon, I hear that you and your family haven't been on a real vacation in five years." Stane reached over and opened a cabinet drawer and retrieved a packet of papers. "I'd like to offer you a special holiday gift this year – a trip to Tahiti for you and your family!" He handed the packet of airline tickets and travel brochures to Berry.

"That's most generous, but I…"

Stane cut him off. "But Simon, I insist." Something about the hard line of his mouth and his tone of voice told Berry it would be wiser to accept gracefully than to argue.

"Thank you. It's really very… But why?"

"Simon, I'll be honest with you. I need someone who's careful and cautious, on whom I can depend. I need to ensure that no major pieces of legislation, certainly not anything controversial, move from the Senate to the President between now and January 10th. You, young man, keep the keys to the kingdom, so to speak. No legislation gets to the President for signature without first going through you."

Berry wondered what the hell he'd gotten himself into. He was already thankful this was one of the few years when Congress was not threatening to close down the government if a budget wasn't passed. "You want me to somehow, um, *lose* legislative bills?"

"No, no. I just want you to slow them down a bit. And only the important bills. You can let minor ones slide, but I need someone to ensure that nothing substantive slips through the cracks. It's holiday season; half of Congress have their minds on mistletoe and fundraising. That means proofreading and reviewing of bills may get sloppy."

"You know I can't just arbitrarily refuse to bring a bill to the White House."

"Not arbitrarily, no. But you can review it for typos, completion, and adherence to all Senate rules."

"Mr. Stane, almost no bill is written perfectly. I mean, they try, but…"

"You want to know my agenda, Simon? I'll tell you. I've been waiting for years for an anti-abortion bill, and the weasels up on the Hill have successfully avoided writing one. I'm out of patience. I know I can't prevent all bills from being signed into law forever, but I think I can hold things up long enough that the Senate Majority Leader will know I mean business." Stane read Berry's face and realized the young man was not yet on board. "It's just one small favor, a temporary one at that." Stane reached into his jacket pocket and pulled out a check for $50,000. He handed it to Berry. "Here's a little spending money for your family while they're in Tahiti."

The first week of December, Senate Bill 1714, unofficially known as the Road Kill Bill, was delivered to the Office of the Executive Clerk so it could be brought to the President and signed into law. Simon Berry began scanning the bill's pages. It seemed unimportant -- a bill relevant mainly to the people of North Dakota. Berry had no qualms taking the Tahiti vacation and cash, all things being morally blurry on the Beltway. But he had a healthy fear of Stane, so he decided to skim the bill, just in case.

He scanned its brief text; no problem. But there was an 18-page amendment on this 3-page bill. He'd better check that out. And guess what? That amendment definitely

would have qualified the Road Kill Bill as 'significant'--
exactly what Bayne Stane had prohibited.

The Road Kill Bill was dead.

Long live the caribou.

Chapter 17

It was the time of year when Santa stocks up on chimney lube. Fewer people bustled through White House corridors, even Beltway traffic seemed less kludgy.

Peabody's personal cell rang as he reviewed an economic proposal. He would have blown off the call if it had come from an adjudicator maneuvering for a Supreme Court appointment, or an irate teamster boss, or the Ambassador to Spain. But his phone indicated the call came from the admin office of the Winooku Indian reservation.

Mohiinok spoke in a wheezy growl. "Nephew, your daughter... Know you are worried about her..." A wretched bronchial cough overtook him. When he recovered, he said, "Took shaman journey last full moon. Saw many things. Allies of the great Manitou will protect your daughter."

"Well, thank you, Uncle. That's, uh, reassuring. But are you all right?" The President listened while Mohiinok liberated more phlegm. "Would you like to spend Christmas at the White House? I could make you comfortable here, and maybe get a doctor to help with that cough."

"You make body comfortable but not spirit." He hacked a few more times. "Wiingezin," he offered a traditional Ojibwa sign-off to his nephew as he hung up.

Chief of Staff Roger Shellish allowed his secretary to pin a tiny penguin wearing ice skates to his lapel in an effort to appear festive.

"The marzipan reindeer that disappeared from the gingerbread house? You asked me to check into it, remember?" his secretary reminded him. The official White House gingerbread house weighed 300 lbs. but apparently suffered a reindeer deficit. "Sarantha was the culprit. She kept sneaking them. She *loves* marzipan."

Roger Shellish chuckled as he adjusted his suit jacket. "No problem. I'll have the baker make extra."

Shellish's secretary slipped into her coat and tied her scarf around her neck. "Thanks for approving my vacation time. Anything else before I leave?"

"The young staffers who were caught caroling down in the bunker?"

"Agent Firth confined them to the press kitchen until they sober up. They'll be fine."

"The fire in the Cabinet Room?"

"The Yule Log was too big for the firebox. Secretary Sutton's pants were scorched by a few embers, but otherwise no damage. The world's still in one piece, Roger. Relax and celebrate." She gave him a quick motherly hug. "Merry Christmas."

The President had invited him to the residence for a drink. Shellish entered the Lincoln Sitting Room where Peabody was involved in intricate negotiations with Royal

158

Lochnager Scotch. "Come on in, Roger!" The President poured his Chief of Staff a generous shot of the amber liquid and raised his own glass. "Happy holidays!"

Roger returned the gesture, then sipped his Scotch slowly, savoring the mellow burn. "Did you watch the Army-Navy game, sir?"

"When Knotts caught that winning touchdown pass; well, damn! Made me wish I could run the government with the same precision he runs a slant route through the secondary!" Peabody stood, walked over to the tall windows and gazed out. The late afternoon sky wore kid's pajamas – puffy cumulus clouds splotched on cerulean blue flannel. Good weather; her flight should be on time. Peabody poured a refill for Roger and himself.

"You seem particularly happy about the holidays this year, sir," Roger remarked, letting the Lochnager sting his palate.

Peabody sat back down and looked at Roger's spiky red hair, eyeglasses, and sincere, open face. Roger uncannily resembled Mr. Peabody's Boy Sherman, an oddity the President would have been happy to point out, if his own name hadn't been Peabody. No need to invite Mr. Peabody-in-the-White-House jokes. "Demmy's coming. She'll be here in a few hours."

"Ah! Will she be staying at the White House, sir?"

She hadn't stayed at the White House since he'd been President. She'd flown into D.C. a few times, in summer and for Sarantha's birthday. But she'd stayed in hotels. He took her willingness to stay in the White House this time as a good omen. "You mean, do we need to advise

159

Press Secretary Fondew she may be grilled about why the President is sleeping with his old girlfriend?"

Roger blushed and swirled the whiskey in his glass.

Peabody continued. "No need to tell Fondew anything. It's the holidays; no one cares." He sipped more Lochnager.

Roger replied softly, "You care, sir."

A wave of empathy hit the President as he realized how difficult it must be for Roger to discuss matters of the heart. Married at 30, he'd lost his wife two years later from cervical cancer. He hadn't remarried. He didn't even date much, preferring to dedicate himself to his work. "Yes, I care." After a pause, the President added, "I hope you won't be alone for the holidays."

"My old college roommate is flying in from Chicago for a visit."

"Well, I'm glad you'll have company." The President's forebrain relaxed in the warmth of Lochnager. He leaned forward and pinched the bridge of his nose for a moment. "Demmy is wicked smart and wicked stubborn. She's never been easy. But when we're together, it feels absolutely right."

" 'Right,' sir?"

" 'Right' as in pandas don't mate with antelope; it doesn't work. Pandas mate with other pandas. She's right for me. Some things you just can't explain."

"All this panda talk makes me wonder if you're planning a new diplomatic overture with Beijing." Roger's humor loosened the intensity of the conversation. Roger sat quietly, leaving the question he'd love to ask hanging silently in the air.

Peabody and Lochnager decided to answer it. "She wanted someone more ambitious."

Roger nearly dropped his glass. "Being President of the United States isn't ambitious enough?"

"I wasn't President when Demmy and I were together. I was in the House. She left me when I refused to run for a third term and took the job at the think tank."

"Why didn't you want a third term?"

"Because it only took two terms to realize my cynicism about government was justified. I don't like tilting at windmills."

"They say most cynics are really crushed romantics."

"Emphasis on 'crushed.'"

Roger stood up and extended his hand. "Thank you for the drink, sir. Merry Christmas."

So far the Christmas season had been the stuff of TV movies and Currier and Ives engravings. They'd taken Sarantha to Annapolis to see the harbor parade of lights, an event that delighted them all. And for a change, his gift to Sarantha had been a hit. He'd gotten her a Sunfish sailboat.

She probably wouldn't sail much while he was President, but as soon as they returned to a normal life, one where they weren't in danger of inhaling a Secret Service agent, Peabody could envision Sarantha enjoying her independence as well as the technical challenges of sailing.

Sarantha seemed happier and less contrary lately. When his daughter asked permission to stay with a friend on New Year's Eve, he'd acquiesced. He had his own plans.

His time with Demmy invigorated his sense of hope. He felt such deep respect for this woman. Her suntanned skin showed weathering from years of medical field work, but good genes, intelligence, and a compassionate nature made her seem even more beautiful, rather than aged. Her courage could only be played on a bass, where the deepest notes resonate. Their bodies still bound together with familiar comfort and seasoned chemistry. As he watched her sleep in the morning light in her soft peach nightgown, he decided to go through with it.

Peabody had requested the marble-topped table in the center of the Blue Room be removed. He had the rug rolled up and carried out, and the wood floor brightly polished. The blue walls, blue Empire chairs emblazoned with golden eagle medallions, the ornate French chandelier and elegant drapes, the fireplace, the relative distance from White House staff, and the feminine oval shape of the room made it his selection for the best place to woo his woman. He had Bose speakers discreetly hidden around the room and a play list of songs at the ready.

"Embrace me, my sweet embraceable you/ Embrace me, you irreplaceable you."

Peabody pulled her closer as they moved together to Gershwin.

She leaned her cheek against his. "I like your cologne," she whispered.

"Bottles for sale in the lobby, just $4.95."

"Oh, you!" she jokingly scolded.

They danced to *Someone To Watch Over Me* and *I Can't Stop Loving You*. When the melodies had worked their magic, he took Demmy's hand and walked her over to what looked like a window. He unsnapped locks on the window ledge, and revealed a jib door which he opened, allowing them to walk out onto the South Portico. There they gazed quietly at the night sky. Peabody took her hand and dropped down on one knee.

"Demmy, we love one another and have for many years. We have a child together. Please, marry me?" He slipped his hand into his trouser pocket to retrieve the ring. He accidentally grabbed the English Bobbie whistle.

She laughed when she saw it, and after an awkward moment, so did he.

He returned the whistle to his pocket and presented the ring. He'd chosen a simple, elegant platinum band with three brilliant stones. "They're not blood diamonds," he assured her. "Read the inscription." He watched her face soften ever so slightly as she turned the band to read 'Love Without Borders' in calligraphy.

"Oh, Sam. I ..."

He rose from his kneeling position. "Did you know that the only President ever to marry in the White House had the ceremony right here in the Blue Room?"

"No, Blue Room history isn't my bailiwick. But I can tell you that blue lips are a sign of..." She looked at his face. "I wish we'd had more dances before things got..."

"Too real? Too serious? Too romantic?"

"All of the above."

"Come on, Demmy. You can't possibly doubt my love for you at this point. And one of these days you're going to wake up in some hut in a third world nation scratching at jungle rot, smelling raw sewage, and you'll realize the world will never run out of sick babies. Never. The world will never run out of people who care and people who don't care. Then maybe wanting to spend time with a husband and daughter who love you won't seem so terrible after all."

"What a charming proposal."

"Have I gotten better with practice? It's been sixteen years. I figure that's enough time for you to change your mind."

"Sam, you're still you; I'm still me. And one of us has to have ambition. One of us has to try –I mean, really try -- to make the world a better place."

"I'm President of the United States, Demmy. I'm doing things to make the world a better place."

Demmy looked at him steadily. "What 'things' are you doing? Just because I was overseas doesn't mean I didn't follow the news, Sam. Congress hasn't passed anything worthwhile except continuing resolutions instead of an actual budget. Social security has been looted by the very government you run, yet nothing's being done to restore the funds. Wealth inequality is ever greater. The too-big-to-fail banks haven't been reined in. And every few months a mentally ill lone wolf guns down a dozen people, or a terrorist wearing a suicide vest walks into a cafe. People are filled with fear, Sam, and they need real leadership. You're not leading. You're treading water, hoping like hell that Washington will survive until your Vice President can run."

"Jesus, Demmy, you can be such a buzz kill!" Peabody paced back and forth for a moment. "OK, maybe I'm not the strongest President the U.S. has ever seen. But even Lincoln or FDR would have trouble working with this Congress." He reached out, took her hand, and drew her close to him with a dance twirl. With their bodies only inches apart, he murmured, "This is me you're talking to, Dem. Me, not some Beltway bloviator. And I don't think this is really about my lack of ambition. I think it's about your father's cheating and what that did to your sense of trust."

She pulled away from him. "A pleasure to meet you, Dr. Freud. Or is it Frazier Crane?"

"I'm serious." Peabody lowered his voice to a whisper. "It scares me that you can pull away from people and relationships as easily as you do. There's something unnatural about how you can yank feelings right out, roots and all. Maybe that's it; maybe you're really incapable of growing roots."

"I have roots. They just don't have all those clinging tendrils."

"Kind of begs the purpose of roots, doesn't it?" But the door to the Blue Room had already shut.

Part III: Battle of Yorktown

Chapter 18

That winter, the temperatures weren't extremely cold; the chill to be felt was in the hearts of Americans. Democrats mocked anyone who identified as Republican. Republicans mocked Democrats and President Peabody, whom they apparently forgot had been their own nominee. When people looked up from their cell phones, they only wanted to socialize with people who held the same worldview they had. They assessed this by sweatshirt logos, iPod playlists, bumper stickers, number of piercings, and sometimes, sadly, the color of another's skin.

Rural America talked football, politics, and soybean prices at the grange after trying to figure out how to pay the combine loan as well as the vet's bill. Residents of urban areas had more options for play yet fewer impulses to do so. Cities festered with human and drug trafficking, hair-trigger racial tension, and the hissing mockery of lost opportunities. None of that contributed a single spark to the fires of love Martin Luther King had tried so hard to kindle.

That winter, the country did not prosper. It endured. That winter, a section of the Schuylkill Expressway in Philadelphia –its concrete warped and twisted by winter cold –buckled, causing a massive traffic jam as well as fatalities. That winter, a depressed celebrity cook used his 7-inch Santoku to slice his own throat on live TV. That winter, angry folks continued to amass weapons, ammunition, food, and supplies in underground bunkers. That winter, the national debt rose to $20 trillion; Standard and Poor's downgraded the U. S. credit rating for the second time in history. That winter, even Hollywood seemed sluggish, offering up a mediocre Oscar season. When the Road Kill Bill (and its Make Regs Make Sense amendment) disappeared from the American political landscape shortly before Christmas, the Peeps, like most Americans, had little oxygen left in their tanks.

If they were to accomplish something even close to a second American revolution, the Peeps needed more effective tactics and a jalapeño pep talk. A few weeks later a news item on TV, in newspapers, and in blogs being discussed all over the country inspired Glenda.

SUPREME COURT APPEAL 'WEDS'
CITIZENS UNITED WITH GAY MARRIAGE

January 10, 20XX. Attorneys representing activist April DeLeon have petitioned the U.S. Supreme Court to grant a Writ of Certiorari to review her case, State of New Jersey v. DeLeon. Last September DeLeon, a resident of Princeton, applied for a marriage license in the Mercer County Courthouse. The name appearing in the Spouse box of her application was 'Articles of Incorporation for Handjob, Inc.' Handjob is a small corporation specializing in artisan-made gifts sold over the internet. The marriage application was denied, and DeLeon appealed the decision all the way to the State Supreme Court, which found the case to be without merit. Now DeLeon hopes the U. S. Supreme Court will take a fresh look. Ms. DeLeon claims to have been inspired by Marin County activist Jonathan Frieman who made a potent legal argument in 2013 that driving his vehicle in the carpool lane with Articles of Incorporation on the passenger's seat was driving with a second 'person,' and therefore legally permitted. Mr. Frieman's attorneys argued that the Supreme Court ruled corporations were people and were entitled to protections under the Bill of Rights. Frieman's case was eventually dismissed, but the non-profit Common-SensibleLaws.org has provided legal and financial assistance to Frieman and others willing to stir the hornet's nest on actions related to Citizens United. DeLeon's attorney stated that her client seeks to explore the limits of U.S. v. Windsor, the Supreme Court decision of June 2013 in which the Defense of Marriage Act was ruled unconstitutional. In a candid statement, Ms. DeLeon admitted, "If a corporation is entitled to the Bill of Rights protection of free speech, how long before a corporation is entitled to the pursuit of happiness which will surely include the right to marry? I want to see the Supreme Court squirm under the weight of its own stupidity." A spokesperson for the U. S Supreme Court said the Court is under no obligation to hear the case. The Supreme Court receives well over 5,000 petitions each year for Writs of Certiorari, but hears only about 125 cases.

Glenda arranged an online chat room meeting on a
Sunday in mid-January. An hour before the meeting, she
received a rejection letter from a private school where she'd
applied to teach. It was hard to start over after 50. She
barely allowed herself a sniffle before she threw herself into
Peeps business. She dabbed Vaseline on the wild sprigs of
her right eyebrow, and let her fingers fly efficiently over the
keyboard as she entered her first message.

Glenda: Happy New Year, folks. I hope you all had
good holidays. As some of you may know, DeVille had a
cardiac episode on Christmas Eve. His doctors have
hospitalized him for some tests, but he thinks he'll be able
to join us online.

Navya, sipping tea and savoring cannoli in the
sunroom of her San Diego home, logged into the chat room
on her iPad. A steady gray rain fell, blurring the view
through the sunroom windows onto her garden. She noticed
movement in her peripheral vision. She saw an attractive
dark-haired man slipping through the oleander. Surely she
imagined it? She and her husband had spent an evening at
the Sycuan Casino about a week ago. Maybe this person's
face subliminally imprinted on her memory. After all, there
couldn't really be a Native American hiding in the bushes of
her backyard in the rain, could there?

Raven: Hi, everyone! Will and I just returned from a
day at Venice Beach. We saw a woman wearing purple
Spandex, a camouflage-print cape, and a small fiddle
hanging from a chain around her neck! She rollerbladed up
and down the boardwalk reciting lines from Ginsburg's
poem Howl.

Glenda: Ah, America! Nice to know freedom of
expression is still alive and well.

170

Vivi: It better be!

Glenda: Are you still in Reykjavik?

Vivi: My parents made me return to Texas for the rest of the school year. Iceland's a country *muy fascinante*. Small but powerful. Einar taught me a lot.

Glenda wondered how Vivi's parents felt about some of the things Einar had probably taught their teenage daughter. She resisted moralizing.

Glenda: Welcome back. Emery, are you here?

Emery: "Yes, hi, Glenda; blessings, everyone. I'm here but may have to leave the chat room early. One of the prisoners I counsel is having a crisis episode. I think he's stabilized for now, but if they call me, I'll have to go."

Glenda: "Understood."

Ted: Hello, all! I flew my girlfriend to a ski lodge this weekend. I've got my Coors and you've got my full attention, at least until Sherry returns. Right now she's changing from ski clothes to something sexier. Women sure change clothes a lot. She's meeting her friend for dinner while I grab a burger and connect with you. Now how are we going to turn Make Regs Make Sense into law?

Emery, Vivi, Navya, Ted, and Raven typed cyber welcomes to one another, and Glenda began the beguine.

Glenda: Looking back over our efforts, I realized luck played in our favor when we slipped R&D money for Fricking into the energy bill. We didn't have as much luck with Make Regs Make Sense. In fact, we were victims of the most pernicious influence in U.S. politics – money.

Ted: You want to get rid of money in politics? Come on, Glenda. That's like getting rid of ticks in the woods.

Emery: Glenda's right. As long as the temptation is there, people will behave in ways that benefit them. Greed is a part of human nature, or at least human nature unredeemed by God's grace.

Raven: Not much grace in Congress.

Emery: More's the pity.

Glenda: Anyway, fellow Peeps --I owe you an apology. I tried to push the Make Regs Make Sense bill through using mostly legitimate channels. But until we fix the root causes of government dysfunction, those channels won't work. 'There are a thousand hacking at the branches of evil to one who is striking at the root.'-Thoreau.

Ted: I get it. It's like trying to do an alignment on a car with a bent axle. No matter how hard you try, you can't get the proper alignment until you replace the axle.

Glenda: Exactly. So I'd like to suggest a good first step. I'm sure you all saw the news articles about the Supreme Court hearing another case related to Citizens United?

She posted a link to one of the articles.

DeVille sat up in his hospital bed in New Orleans. He moved an IV line out of the way, asked a nurse for help with his laptop, then he logged in. DeVille: What's this Cit United thing all about?

While the other Peeps greeted him, Glenda provided the Reader's Digest version.

172

Glenda: In 2010 the Supreme Court heard a legal case called Citizens United versus the Federal Election Commission. They decided corporations are not only 'persons' for legal purposes, but that since they are persons, they have protection under the Bill of Rights. The bottom line was that corporations could give pretty much whatever money they want to further their interests. They donate the money through organizations called SuperPacs.

DeVille: So that's what a SuperPac is. Thought it had something to do with the NFL. These judges said corporations are people? Don't sound right to me. I can sprinkle powdered sugar on meatloaf. Don't make it a beignet. How do we get Sup Ct to fix this?

Glenda: The best way to go about it is to amend the Constitution. The amendment would overturn the Citizens United court decision.

Navya: Why do we want to abridge the rights of corporations? American businesses operate in a competitive environment. Why shouldn't they be able to give money to support their interests? They pay taxes.

Glenda reached down to give Socrates the Havanese a doggie treat. She thought for a moment. Glenda: Businesses are made up of humans and human citizens already have the right to free speech. But it's not an unlimited right. You can't yell "Fire!" in a crowded theater. Your free speech is limited so you don't harm others. And there are limits to how much any citizen can donate to a political candidate or cause. If corporations donate huge amounts of money to the political process, they harm the democratic voting power of others. Giving corporations personhood and protection of the Bill of Rights is a form of corporatism, not capitalism. And you're a capitalist, right?

173

Navya: Of course I'm a capitalist!

Raven: We're just ordinary people. We tried to accomplish big things; we got lucky with a few. But maybe we've gone far enough?

Ted: No way, Raven! Your green energy project got funded. The rest of us still want to whip this government into shape." Ted chugged his Coors and made quick work of a double-cheeseburger. Good thing his fellow Peeps couldn't smell the onions across cyberspace.

Raven: Just trying to be realistic.

Emery: Let's get down to it, folks. I have to lead a Bible study group in twenty minutes.

Glenda: OK. People have been trying to pass a Constitutional amendment to overturn Citizens United for years. We'll join in on existing efforts, and we'll also raise the ante. I have assignments for all of you.

DeVille – follow doctor's orders

Raven – Special Ops.

Vivi –manage all computer issues and keep our communication secure/private.

Ted – Special Ops.

Navya – Coordinate with existing organizations like MovetoAmend.org, EndCitizensUnited.org, and the one mentioned in the recent news articles, Common-SensibleLaws.org. Join these organizations, find out what road blocks they're hitting, and report back.

And I'll write another blog.

Immediately Peeps fingers went flying. "What's 'Special Ops'?"

Glenda: I'll do research and Navya will report what barriers these organizations have identified. Between them and us, we'll figure out who needs some "Peeps persuasion" to help them get on-board to overturn Citizens United. We'll focus on power players – committee chairs, high-ranking members of the caucuses, the Whips, etc. I'll start my research as soon as I write a new blog. Emery, we may have to bring you into Special Ops for a few things, too. Our methods won't be violent, but they will smell a lot like coercion, so the less the rest of you know, the better.

Glenda waited a few moments until everyone in the chat room had a chance to read her post.

Glenda: DeVille, you need to focus on feeling better. We'll manage without you for a while. But for the rest of you Peeps – it's time to cross the Delaware!

Navya: Getting my oars!

Vivi: I'm in. Einar taught me a lot during the holidays. *No problemas* for me to help out. Fuck this 'corporations are people' *mierda*!

Emery: On board!

Raven: Fired up and ready to go!

Raven thought using Obama's old campaign slogan would bug Ted, but he surprised her.

Ted: Corporations are people, my ass. Let's do it!

175

Five days later, readers of the nation's most popular blogs received a full serving of Glenda with their breakfast coffee.

Once Upon a Time, Citizens Really Were United...Against Corporatism

Once upon a time a young land full of wannabes, third sons, those released from debtors' prisons, dreamers, die-hards and the devout rose up. Their land was ruled by the most powerful empire of the time. King George III of Great Britain provided the face of that empire; British corporations (think shipbuilding, tea, tobacco) provided the money and muscle behind the throne. When King George's administrators imposed taxes on everyday items people needed – things like tea and whiskey – the young country got grumpy. Cobblers, farmers, tavern owners, tailors, blacksmiths, and other ordinary hard-working people started to think about government. About liberty. About justice. About what kind of a nation they wanted. They trusted some decent men to conceive of the ideas and write the documents that would send many of them to die on battlefields of the American Revolution.

By the time we'd earned our freedom from King George, Americans had unambiguously declared to the world that our fledgling government valued the rights of citizens and the liberties of its voters. These new Americans remembered the brutish tactics of Britain's big corporations. They made certain their own corporations would have fewer rights and far less power. American corporations were limited in their participation in politics and were bound by laws designed to allow them to conduct robust business, but not much else.

America prospered under its new mantle until push came to shove on the slavery issue. The founding fathers had ducked that one, and it came back to bite them in the hind quarters. Most of us know the outcomes of the Civil War: the Emancipation Proclamation, the loss of 620,000 lives, carpetbaggers, Reconstruction, and... (wait for it) procurement contracts!

Who did those military procurement contracts go to? Corporations. The Civil War fortified certain businesses. Many profited; some profiteered. After the Civil War corporations had so much money they 'bought' judges, senators, and other officials without shame.

In 1886 a Supreme Court case upped the ante. It agreed to hear Santa Clara County v. Southern Pacific Railroad, a case about a railroad properties tax. In a head note [similar to a sidebar], a court reporter gave his opinion on how the Supreme Court interpreted the equal protection clause of the Fourteenth Amendment as it related to corporations. The reporter wrote that the Supreme Court considered a private corporation a "natural person." The note actually said more about the reporter's understanding than it did about any judicial doctrine. It may have begun as a mistake but it was one the Court never corrected. And that, my fellow Americans, is how corporations became people.

Naturally, corporations were delighted. And just as naturally, ordinary American citizens went about raising children, harvesting the corn, teaching school, or running the deli, and took no notice that the Supreme Court had just given their democracy a Brazilian wax job.

Give corporations free rein and they will grow. They will multiply. They will eat each other's young. By the early 20th century, corporations employed nearly 80% of the country's non-farm laborers. The business of America was business. Teddy Roosevelt did what he could to break up the corporations holding monopolies (trusts) on certain industries. But over time corporate lawyers found ways around many of his trust-busting techniques. Local, state, and federal courts, as well as the Supreme Court favored corporations rather than individuals in their rulings.

In the 1950s racial unrest rocked the deep South. The N.A.A.C.P. and C.O.R.E (Congress of Racial Equality) had been legally organized as corporations. When Black lives were lost during civil rights protests, those organizations sought protection for their members for the rights of free speech and assembly. This led courts to strengthen and uphold the notion that corporations, as persons, deserved protection under the Bill of Rights.

In 2007 the Supreme Court heard another case, this one from an advocacy group, Wisconsin Right to Life. That decision castrated campaign finance reform and opened the floodgates for corporations to give virtually unlimited amounts of money to SuperPacs associated with a particular issue without having to disclose who was giving what to whom. This "dark money" is not raised or spent by any political candidate or party. It's money raised and spent by billionaire multinational corporations standing above the candidates, holding the puppet strings.

Think about that.

Once upon a time, citizens were united – against corporatism. Is it any wonder that a New Jersey woman now wants to know if corporate 'persons' have the right to pursue happiness and walk down the aisle with the spouse of their choice? Let's hope the Supreme Court hears this case with new ears and with a heightened sense of democracy.

We're the Peeps and we're taking back our nation.

Chapter 19

The Peeps' research identified several Congressional power players who consistently voted against amending the Constitution to abrogate Citizens United, but only two had usable vulnerabilities: Senator Henry Lacomb and House Majority Whip Benjamin Prunapart. The "Special Ops" kicked in.

At 9:00 PM on a January night, silhouettes of leafless tree limbs lent an eeriness to the suburban Virginia cul de sac lined with multi-million dollar homes. Ted checked the street to make sure Representative Prunapart and his younger wife (by 27 years) were nowhere on the grounds. He crept from behind a hedge on Prunapart's property, carrying a small toolbox. He used a pocket laser to deactivate the home security system. With the lock-picking tools DeVille had recently taught him to wield, he unlocked the side door into the Prunapart's garage and went to work.

Five days ago during a downpour of rain, Mrs. Prunapart, an ex-Miss Romania, left her new Mercedes S-class sedan in an underground parking garage while she went to the dentist. Disguised as a mobile oil change technician, Ted drained the car's windshield wiper fluid and replaced it with motor oil, ensuring slimed windows on the $100K vehicle. Three days ago he'd hidden the carcass of a dead pigeon underneath the rear passenger seat. The smell was horrid – exactly as the Peeps hoped it would be.

Glenda's instructions had been to sabotage the car as often and as thoroughly as possible without endangering anyone's life. After researching the auto's specifications and vulnerabilities, Ted had special-ordered a diagnostic override device with wireless capacity, and had it shipped to his motel room. He now had the means for creating the kind of automotive havoc Glenda wanted. The device would allow him wireless control of the auto's lights, steering, brakes, sound system, seat belts, windshield wipers and air-conditioning. He reached into his jacket pocket and retrieved the device which resembled a flash drive on steroids. He located the car's hidden diagnostic port and connected the device. The sleek silver sedan would be under his control for the foreseeable future, at least until a mechanic with common sense looked at it.

And then, as Glenda had instructed, he left a typed letter on the front passenger seat. Glenda had paid a Sous Chef from the Romanian Embassy to translate it, explaining it was for a work of fiction. Glenda hoped there were no recipes tucked between the lines.

Mrs. Anca Albescu Prunapart,

Like you, I am immigrant from Juc-Herghelie area. You left Romania and made a comfortable life for yourself here in America. But some of us who immigrated have not done so well. It's harder and harder for those of us who moved to the U.S. in search of a better life to be able to find one. Your husband, a Congressman, fights to uphold the Citizens United decision which only serves interests of rich, depriving working class immigrants of opportunities. Fifty of your fellow Romanians have joined me in placing an ancient Romanian curse on your transportation until you persuade your husband to overturn Citizens United. You are beautiful Romanian woman; you should know how to make your husband happy so he will do this small favor for you. No car on earth will work well for you until curse is lifted. You know this. You owe this to your people.

We will remove curse when we see your husband change his position. We'll know when, and if, that happens.

Dumitru Petri

Ted chuckled at the idea of a Romanian folk curse causing the Mercedes' problems, but Glenda had done her research and was certain the ex-beauty queen was not the sharpest tack in the shed. He was pretty certain Prunapart's eye candy would be utterly convinced of the curse's power.

He left the letter on the driver's seat and relocked the vehicle. Wiping his finger prints from the car's hood and door handles with a cloth, he and his tool box slipped from the garage as covertly as they had entered. The half moon shining through clouds made those bare tree limbs look even spookier.

Several days later, Raven received her marching orders from Glenda via the secure chat room.

Glenda: Senator Lacomb is a doting grandfather with only one grandchild, a boy named Mirth. Lacomb desperately wants to get his grandson into an extremely exclusive private school, the Columbia Youth Academy in Georgetown. Little Mirth has been on their waiting list since he was a week old. I think Lacomb would wheel and deal on Citizens United if he thought it would guarantee his grandson's placement at the school.

Raven: They really named the kid 'Mirth?'

Glenda: Go figure. Lacomb's daughter was a free-spirited earth-child who now writes the Beltway Boogie blog. She's caused him problems over the years. The kid's father is a musician-wannabe. Lacomb figures if the kid doesn't get the best private school education possible, he'll turn out to be a shipwreck. Or worse, a liberal.

Raven: How am I supposed to get Lacomb's grandson into this la-di-da school?

Glenda: That's the brilliance of it -- you don't need to! Vivi already hacked the school's computers. She learned he's been accepted on a preliminary basis for the first year of kindergarten. But Lacomb doesn't know that. Vivi deleted Mirth's acceptance letter from their mailing list. You will play the role of a school board trustee with a Citizens United agenda. Vivi's already substituted your headshot for the photo of the real trustee on the school's website.

Raven sat in a Beltway restaurant the Friday before the Super Bowl, waiting for Senator Lacomb. Not wanting to get lost around Dupont Circle à la Sydney Wade, Raven allowed herself extra time and arrived early. She ordered a virgin margarita and carefully blotted her lipstick after each sip. She wore her best suit, her Rodeo Drive blouse, and the only pair of Manolo Blahniks she owned. Glenda believed she could pull this off, but Raven herself wasn't so sure. Wouldn't being a half Black, half Hispanic woman be a barrier to impersonating a trustee on the board of a snobby private school? And wasn't Lacomb one of the most powerful members of the Senate? How the heck did she think she'd handle that dawg?

Moments later Senator Lacomb approached her table, nodded a greeting, and sat down. Raven immediately knew she was on a fool's errand. As a woman of color, she recognized his subtle body language, the refusal to make eye contact, the disappointment revealed in his facial muscles. The man was a racist. Overturning Citizens United was important, but Glenda would have to think of something else. Raven would go through the motions but she already knew this was pointless.

Lacomb looked around and motioned for a server. He ordered for both of them without consulting Raven. "Ms. Endicott, what's your concern?"

"It's about your grandson, Mirth, and his application for acceptance into Columbia Youth Academy."

Lacomb leaned across the restaurant table eagerly. "Yes?"

"As you may know, I'm on the board of trustees. I have influence."

"Yes, yes, your phone message indicated as much. How can I help you?"

A waiter delivered a Manhattan on the rocks to the Senator. Raven waited until he'd had a several sips. Couldn't hurt to loosen him up before she made her pitch. But a TV set over the restaurant bar caught everyone's attention. Servers stopped in their tracks, arms loaded with plate-filled trays. Patrons twisted in their chairs to watch and listen as CNN broadcast its news feed.

I read the news today, oh boy…

Senator Lacomb listened, too, and in less than 30 seconds, his cell rang. Abruptly, he excused himself from their luncheon date. He had urgent business to attend to.

Chapter 20

An Hour Earlier, the Same Day

Inside the White House Briefing Room, Press Secretary Fondew stood behind the podium which had been lowered to accommodate her 5' 2" stature. In front of her was a gaggle of microphones. Behind her stood two men and one woman.

"Good morning, ladies and gentlemen of the fourth estate!" She began the daily press briefing. "The President's schedule today includes a meeting with Republican National Committee leadership. That meeting is…" Fondew glanced at the wall clock at the back of the Press Briefing Room. "…in progress right now. This afternoon President Peabody will meet with the Secretary of Health and Human Services." She cleared her throat and continued. "That meeting was scheduled due to the President's concern about misinformation reaching the public on the subject of autism. I have here with me today…" she turned her head slightly toward the men and gave the woman behind her a half-wink. "…Dr. Hamilton Hunt of the American Autism Society, Dr. Kenneth Spietz of the American Psychological Association, and Dr. Nancy Fondew, the Director of the Center for Neurological Research. And yes, we're related. She's my sister-in-law."

She continued. "As you no doubt are aware, some have theorized that vaccines are responsible for the apparent increase in the diagnostic rate for autism and associated disorders in the United States. Children who are not

185

vaccinated pose a public health risk, so these theories are taken seriously." She paused for emphasis, then enunciated crisply, "These theories have been scientifically debunked."

President Peabody pushed his chair back from the Roosevelt Room conference table around which were gathered members of the GOP leadership. They were there to formulate a plan for the next Presidential election cycle. They assumed he didn't want to run. But the party leadership was not at all sure Vice President Athena Storm would please the oligarchy segment of their constituency. They wanted to discuss options.

Peabody had eaten his favorite breakfast – oatmeal pancakes with fresh sliced peaches -- and had watched a lively interview with Jake Lee, one of the quarterbacks who would compete in the Super Bowl. He'd had a non-alarming daily security briefing, and had exchanged a devilishly funny joke with Roger Shellish. Press Secretary Fondew was educating citizens about autism in the Briefing Room, a mission he'd personally assigned to her. His day had gone about as well as possible, so far, for a President.

Reluctant to rain (or pee) on his own parade, he allowed himself to daydream throughout the GOP leadership meeting while staring at the Rough Rider portrait of Teddy Roosevelt. His inattentiveness didn't matter. They didn't really care what he said or thought; it was a formality that they included him. He was a placeholder President and the party leadership never let him forget it.

The meeting was about to wrap when Shellish appeared in the doorway. "Mr. President, I need to see you, sir." Something in his tone transmitted that Roger wasn't going to ask him to explain the punch line of the morning's joke.

The two men huddled close together in the White House hallway. Shellish's hands trembled as he referred to a handwritten note. "Mr. President ..."

Back in the Briefing Room, Press Secretary Fondew was on a roll. "Recently Pastor Lance Huckleberry of the Glory Be Church in San Angelo, Texas issued controversial statements linking the incidence of autism to American tolerance of gays and lesbians. While medical research does not yet have all the answers on autism and related disorders, there is no evidence that the presence of gay and lesbian persons in a culture correlates to the number of ..."

President Peabody entered the Briefing Room. He exchanged a look with his Press Secretary. She immediately moved aside and offered him the microphone.

Peabody approached the podium and looked out over the press corps. He held a hand over his mouth briefly while his other hand fidgeted with the Bobbie whistle in his slacks pocket. He seemed to be trying to come to terms with something. After a moment, he addressed the room. "Approximately fifteen minutes ago, a private jet carrying the Portland Loggers football team to the Super Bowl exploded and crashed over eastern Wyoming. Seventy-eight people were on board – 53 players as well as coaches, support staff, pilots and crew. All are presumed dead." The President paused, swallowing hard. "I don't have many details yet. The Director of National Intelligence confirmed that ISIS has taken credit for sabotaging the plane on Al Jazeera. Press Secretary Fondew will brief you throughout the day as more information becomes available. Thank you."

Peabody hurried back to the Oval Office where he spent three intense hours in the Situation Room consulting with Homeland Security, the Director of National Intelligence, his Transportation Secretary, and the Joints Chiefs. By late afternoon, a solid piece of intelligence led FBI agents to two suspects living in a suburb of Portland. The intensity of focus gave Peabody a headache that felt like someone had pierced his eyeballs with knitting needles. He disbanded the meeting while they awaited further information on the interrogation of the suspects, and directed Shellish to get his limo ready.

"Where to, Mr. President?"

"I don't know yet, Roger, but I have to get out of here, even if it's just for a little while. I don't know if it makes any sense, but I need to be among the people. Ordinary people."

"Yes, Mr. President."

Peabody ducked into the White House residence, changed into a pair of jeans, a black pullover, a jacket and a ball cap. Ten minutes later he was being driven through Beltway traffic. He ordered the driver to drop him off at a crowded pub. He asked the two Secret Service agents accompanying him to let him blend in with the crowd as much as possible. Peabody walked around the bar, eavesdropping as customers responded to the news blasting on TV.

"Un-frickin-believable! How did ISIS get access to the Loggers' jet?"

"They would have beaten the Vikings at the Super Bowl. Those guys had so much talent!"

"Damn, why didn't we elect Hrump when we had the chance? This would never have happened on his watch. Peabody's almost as bad as Obama."

"Jake Lee was the finest quarterback I've seen in a decade. I can't believe it. I just can't believe I'll never see him throw a touchdown pass again."

"We should sabotage the planes of all Middle Eastern soccer teams. Except Israel's, of course."

"Football is America. What the hell is this country coming to?"

After a while the President asked to be driven to the Capitol building. With the Secret Service at a distance, he wandered among tourists in the Rotunda, soaking in the immense paintings. He approached the 12' x 18' Declaration of Independence scene by Trumbull. Look at all those pale, middle-aged white men, he thought; talk about politically incorrect! MSNBC would never have approved their homogeneity, and I sure wouldn't want to wear those wigs and stockings on Fox!

He crossed the room and headed for the equally grand Baptism of Pocahontas, the painting he considered the best in the Rotunda. The artist had managed to make the splotches of white --Pocahontas's gown, the priest's vestment, the silky banner, the blinding glints of armor— absolutely gleam. It was both Peabody's favorite and most despised painting in the Rotunda; he supposed that's why it pulled him. He detested the concept of Pocahontas as cultural-appropriator. He hated that she had chosen to turn on her people's ways to gain respect and safety among

189

white men. And yet, hadn't one of his own grandmothers done exactly that? He loved that the artist, John Gadsby Chapman, had included Pocahontas's uncle Opechancanough in the painting. He sat off to the right, staring into the distance, brooding. Good old uncle O. trusted the conversion as far as he could roll it uphill and would later cause as much trouble as he could for the colonists. Peabody may have been the only modern President to know that Pocahontas was of the Powhatan tribe, and the Powhatan were part of the Algonquian nation. Even though he carried more WASP blood in his veins than Algonquian, Pocahontas moved him.

Peabody stepped back from the painting and scanned the tourists who gawked at the art and read the plaques. A clutch of Scandinavian teens jostled one another. Three white-haired octogenarians stood in line at the water fountain like WalMart greeters who'd found an oasis. A young Korean family examined the Discovery of the Mississippi painting; the girl asked her parents if the gold on the frame around the painting was from Fort Knox. A kindergarten teacher, wearing a polo shirt with a Hebrew and English logo, reminded her charges to hold each another's hand. It was not lost on Peabody that every day, thousands of people just like these came to Washington to ponder the buildings, the documents, the history of the world's most effective and prosperous democracy. Would they still be visiting the Washington Monument, the Jefferson Memorial, the Capitol Rotunda in ten years?

The words of one of the pub patrons stayed in his head: "Football is America. What the hell is this country coming to?"

Football rated right up there with baseball and rock-n-roll as activities that could bring Americans together. The terrorists knew this, and that's exactly why they'd murdered 78 innocents. *Where have you gone, Joe DiMaggio, a nation turns its lonely eyes to you.* Could he, like Joltin' Joe, inspire America's spirit? Cynicism and patience hadn't made Demmy his wife. Cynicism and patience hadn't made America a better nation. Time to change tactics.

The President paced the Oval Office the next day, venting to his Chief of Staff, not truly expecting answers. "Roger, everyone talks about wanting the White House to show real leadership. Don't believe it. Leadership is the last thing they want. Confidence in your own decision-making is the opposite characteristic of those who sit around at meetings, stare into their coffee cups, and collect their $21.50 an hour. Backbone, chutzpah, grit – they're not politically correct. They're individualistic traits in a world where collaboration has become the meme."

Roger Shellish leaned forward in his chair and made a finger-steeple. He started to say something, hesitated, then asked, "I wonder, sir, could it be a matter of sequence? Perhaps a certain kind of leadership must precede collaboration? A good leader would decide which path should be taken. Collaborators could then work on the details – what shoes to wear for the journey, what food to take."

"You're a good man, Roger," Peabody said. He walked over to a table holding a whiskey decanter and poured both of them a shot. He handed one drink to Roger, clinked glasses and sipped. "The party leadership will put my balls in a vice. That leech Festring will go on the radio and call me a coward. Lacomb will push as hard as he can, on behalf of his buddies in oil and gas, to invade another oil-producing country. They want this attack to lead us into a ground war in the Middle East. There's big money behind them, Roger. But I have my own plan in mind. I need to speak with David Nirvidian again. Bring Fondew into the meeting, too. And, do you remember that group of people my daughter got involved with last summer?"

Shellish tilted his head with curiosity and nodded.

"There was a teenage girl – a hacker –in that group. I want her picked up and brought to the White House. It's time she and I had a chat."

Shellish looked both baffled and proud as he headed to his office to make calls.

That evening TV sets delivered the wreckage from Wyoming into America's living rooms. Carry-on bags, helmets, burnt and fractured bones, scorched super-size shoes, iPods, torqued seat cushions, and unidentifiable fragments of what used to be humans were strewn throughout Wyoming's Thunder Basin National Grasslands. The bison, antelope and wolves who lived there kept their distance. The vultures circled overhead.

The media also delivered the news that the Supreme Court refused to grant the writ of certiorari for the State of New Jersey v. DeLeon, on the grounds that the articles of incorporation were different than the corporation itself; therefore, DeLeon could not marry what held 'personhood' i.e., the corporation, and therefore the case had no merit. It cruised right by most people's radar.

The tension on the streets was palpable. ISIS could not murder a football team on its way to the Super Bowl without igniting American ire.

President Basho Samuels Peabody led the next press briefing himself. "Yesterday America experienced a loss greater than we can find words to express. Seventy-eight people – people who had no reason to expect anything but excitement, competition and fun – met their Maker."

"In the grand metaphysical scheme of things, we don't know why such evil happens. We can't really wrap our minds around it. But in the practical everyday understanding of our world, we know exactly what caused this. A jihadi terrorist group appointed itself as judge, jury and executioner on an international scale and decided these people should die."

"ISIS has taken credit for this horrendous act..." Peabody looked up from his notes and saw the press corps hanging on his every word. "...and we will give it to them.

"We have already begun a thorough investigation of how the jet was sabotaged. We've apprehended two suspects and are interrogating them. We will bring the perpetrators to justice. Count on it.

"Second, we will initiate economic sanctions against our ally, Saudi Arabia. You may find this strange. I don't like it much either. But until Saudi Arabia acts like an ally, we have no choice. Economic sanctions, including an oil embargo, will continue until the Saudi Arabian government stops sowing the seeds of terrorism. It does us no good to address specific acts of jihadi terrorism until the Saudi *madrassas* remove the hate-speech against Jews and Christians that currently passes as education. This is non-negotiable."

"Third, I'm asking Congress to approve emergency funding to hire fifty new government forensic accountants.

Their top priority will be to disrupt the flow of funds to ISIS from any and all sources.

"Fourth, we will update and revise the No Fly list so that it's actually useful. If America can put the Rover on Mars, we can create and manage a No Fly list. No one on the list will board an airline into this country, nor will they be allowed to buy weapons in the U.S. If Congress refuses to act, I'll issue an executive order to accomplish this.

"Fifth, I will create a powerful new cyber-security program to detect and track ISIS activity on social media. We'll provide details on that program at a later date.

"In the meantime, know this: America is on the gridiron and we're playing to win."

Chapter 21

Sometimes a girl just needs her mother, Glenda thought, even (or especially) a mother who passed away more than six months ago. She snuggled close to her little dog Socrates. She felt the Mom-impulse Friday night when she returned from a second date with Timothy, a decent guy who worked in biochemistry. On many dates Glenda had dowsed potential by not being able to respond meaningfully when her date referred to the music of the Cocktail Slippers or the sneakers Bruno Mars wore at his last performance. Pop culture had never been Glenda's forté, but Timothy didn't seem to mind. Their interactions had felt promising until that hyper-salivating exercise of the sublingual glands he called a good-night kiss.

But it wasn't just the disappointing date that made Glenda long for her mother's voice. It was the failure to pass Make Regs Make Sense, the Supreme Court's refusal to hear the DeLeon case, the horrific murder of an entire football team, and the short dark days of winter –each of those factors plucked notes in her personal blues. Glenda did not indulge herself often, but she withdrew money from savings, booked a reservation, and flew to Cielo, Florida to a health spa she'd heard about.

Her first day flowed in a vinyasa of sunshine, tropical flowers, Pilates, lemon water, terrycloth robes, rattan, saunas, sweat, and meals -- of adzuki beans, sea buckthorn, star fruit, Romanesco, and teff. The sensations of beauty, comfort and nourishment washed over her.

Alone at night she tried to sleep but thoughts bombarded. Ever since the Supreme Court refused to hear the DeLeon case, no one was talking about Citizens United. It was all terrorism now. Every headline and nearly every conversation concerned ISIS, Saudi Arabia, investigations, the Middle East, and radicals. Raven had made no headway with Senator Lacomb. Ted's Romanian-cursed-car might persuade Prunapart to act, but Capitol Hill simply wasn't paying attention to anything but terrorism. What had she gotten the Peeps, this brave little band of citizens, into? How had she convinced herself they could change the government? How long could this little troupe avoid detection and arrest? And why did she find it so hard to relate to available men her age? Why did life have to be so complicated?

She snorted bitterly with self-awareness. Here she lay with her head on a 600-count freshly laundered pillow case and she thought life was complicated! What must a single mother of three living in a tenement think when her weary head fell at night on a pile of her children's pajamas?

The following day a Zen alarm clock's resonant chimes awakened Glenda. She checked her schedule: yoga, a talk on dream interpretation by an Oprah disciple, bodywork, a bit of unstructured time, a facial, and dinner.

She moved through the early part of her day like a sleepwalker, feeling a passivity she rarely allowed herself. She found the dream interpretation workshop mundane. People dream about unfinished business, sex, and fear: big reveal! She wondered if anyone else in the class dreamed about Congressmen of the 1800's and filling out dating site questionnaires.

196

After lunch Glenda lay in a private treatment room, her slender middle-aged body prone on a massage table. As the bodywork practitioner (who referred to herself as a *lomi lomi*) began to work, Glenda felt her internal resistance rise and fall a number of times. The practitioner used a variety of techniques. A few of them caused mild pain followed by luscious release. Somehow her muscles gradually felt more smoothly entwined with her bones. Layers of tension melted away. The diffuser in the room sent periodic bursts of aroma into the air. "What's this fragrance? I love it."

"Lemon, bergamot, Atlas cedar, and frankincense. Excellent for strengthening, clarifying and purifying."

"If I believed in heaven, this is what it would smell like," Glenda murmured.

The *lomi lomi* began a series of rolling motions on Glenda's lower back. Glenda felt a huge wave of emotion cresting inside her. She told the bodyworker, "That's enough for me now." The *lomi lomi* slipped quietly from the room, granting Glenda privacy.

Later Glenda roamed the women-only section of the spa property. Nudity was permitted there, and a few spa clients took advantage of it. She was not one of them. The expansive grounds were beautifully maintained. Lounge chairs and small teak tables sat in the shade of regal palms. Glenda wandered into a meadow-like area decorated with bronze sculptures of nude women bending, praying, kneeling, and star-gazing, all with graceful lines that suggested organic movement. Glenda approached one particular sculpture, a woman sitting bent over with her forehead close to the ground. Something about the pose, its surrender and its femaleness, burst Glenda's internal dam.

She sat next to the sculpture on the soft grass and cried until she could cry no more.

Late in the afternoon she settled into a private room where she'd scheduled a facial. Glenda endured eyebrow waxing, plucking (ouch!), and pomade, the irritation from which was soothed by hydrocortisone cream. Then came exfoliation, toning, and a mask of some mysterious seaweed and muck mixture. The esthetician gently applied a coconut-scented moisturizer to her face and placed two cucumber slices over Glenda's eyelids. "Rest, and allow your skin to appreciate what you've done for it. You can leave whenever you're ready."

Glenda lay on the treatment table in her thick white robe. Her muscles and tissues felt less tense since the bodywork and the tears, but she still felt adrift. What can I do? How can I guide the Peeps? Can we really accomplish anything? Is overturning Citizens United the best way to address the root causes of corruption in American politics? What do voters really want? What are the American people's real priorities? An old maxim interjected itself into her stream of consciousness: *Show me your checkbook and I'll tell you what you value.*

Glenda sat up suddenly, cucumber slices sliding from her eyelids. Her eyes flashed open wide. Hell, could it really be that simple? She couldn't remember where she heard that quote, but its truth rang clear. People will say they value all kinds of high-minded things, but when it comes down to the nitty gritty of paying for them, values shift. How could the Peeps find the shared values that American citizens agree on? The answer was so simple: Give citizens the power of the purse and see what they are really willing to pay for. Let them vote with their wallets. That's it!

198

In her state of euphoria, Glenda failed to notice the log-like creature moving slowly through the grass twenty feet from her as she walked back to her room.

Suddenly the alligator's jaws opened. Although jogging was not listed as one of the spa's fitness activities, Glenda ran.

Glenda had already spent ten minutes in the Peeps online chat room trying to explain her epiphany. Slowly, they were latching on to it.

Emery: So we'd have some mechanism when we file our income tax that would let us apportion how much of our taxes would go to what purposes?

Glenda: Exactly. You could have your tax payment go to inner city renewal or environmental clean-up. Or if you hate inner city renewal and environmental clean-up, you could direct your tax dollars to science and health research, the military, or to reduce the federal deficit. Shouldn't be too hard to add a page to the income tax filing form to allow tax payers to divvy up their taxes to pay for the things they care about.

Raven: But Glenda, didn't you just persuade us a few weeks ago that Citizens United was the root cause of government dysfunction and that we had to deal with that first? Now you want us to forget Citizens United and move on to some new brainstorm?

Glenda hesitated. She could feel Raven's frustration. Besides, she knew Raven was making a point most of them were already thinking. Glenda began typing: Overturning Citizens United would clean up campaign finance quite a bit

199

and reduce the influence of lobbyists. But why do lobbyists throw money at politicians? Because they want something from them like subsidies, tax cuts, kick backs, sole-source contracts, etc. If we eliminate the middle man –Congress— so that nothing stands between the citizenry and their government's budget, then lobbyists would have to lobby more than a hundred million voters, not just 535 members of Congress. So, yes, Raven, overturning Citizens United would have helped. A lot. But taking back the power of the purse – that could help in practical and inspirational ways.

Navya: How can you expect the government or businesses to create budgets or plan long-term for the future if revenue isn't known until well after April 15th?

Glenda: We'll phase it in gradually over five or ten years. I'll write a brochure explaining the whole idea and get it to all of you.

Raven: We don't even have to be sneaky about this, right?

Glenda: Not at all! We want to be transparent now and push the concept out to the American people. I think the country's ready for it. Nearly all of the ugliest fights in Congress are about budget or appropriations. The House Appropriations Committee has long held pieces of good legislation hostage. They do it because they can; they have the power to say where American dollars go. Why should Congress, an institution with roughly a 10% approval rating --get to write America's budget? Why not let the people do it? So, yes, let's go public!

Vivi: Einar told me when Iceland had its revolution, it was all public and legal. And non-violent. They sentenced 26 corrupt bankers to 74 years in prison! Pretty cool.

Emery: Glenda, you asked me to put you in touch with my brother, the one who went to law school with Peabody's Chief of Staff. Did he help you with your questions?

Glenda: Yes, thanks, Emery. Mainly I was concerned about whether this idea is constitutional.

Ted: Why?

Glenda: Article 1, Section 9 of the Constitution says, "No money shall be drawn from the Treasury, but in Consequence of Appropriations made by Law..."

Ted: Hey, I'm not supporting anything that's against the Constitution!

Glenda: It may or may not be, depending on how judges read the law. Emery's brother said we could tie in the concept of Vote Your Wallet as a freedom of speech concept, like what happened in Citizens United. He recommended we get the legislation passed, and see if anyone challenges it in court. If they do, we pursue it all the way to the Supreme Court. It would be difficult for the judicial branch to take away a privilege if it has strong popular support.

DeVille: I like this idea, Glenda. Been waiting for a chance to get more money for the V.A. and maybe for inner city food gardens.

Glenda: DeVille, I have something special for you – a Happiness Tax Agenda!

DeVille: ???

Glenda: We haven't yet helped you with your essential issue of happiness as a national priority. I did some research. There's a lot of data on what's conducive to a happy society. It's interesting; many of the same factors appear whether you study happiness in Denmark, Japan, Bhutan or India. There's a healthy economy, affinity to nature, community vitality, acceptance of our own mortality, cultural diversity, education, tolerance, effective and affordable health care --even clean toilets play a role. So I'm creating an optional tax prioritization form –the Happiness Agenda-- anyone who wants their money to go toward priorities associated with happiness can use it. And the form could be customized. People could use it as a starting point, then delete things they didn't agree with, or add things they wanted to fund.

DeVille: The pursuit of happiness – yay!! Thank you, cher.

Glenda: Vivi, we'll need your help to program the new tax form.

Vivi: Problem. The President has me involved with anti-terrorism efforts on social media. A bunch of my hacker friends are in on this, too. Can't say any more than that but I won't have time to develop this create-your-own-budget tax form now. My folks are pressuring me about school. *Mierda*! Not even sure I'm gonna graduate. Even with Einar's help, it's been kinda *loco*.

Glenda: Well, our initial work will be to get the country educated and excited about the concept. It'll be a little while before we need more of your time, Vivi.

Ted: What do I, as a Tea Party member, get out of this new idea of yours?

Glenda: Exactly what every voter gets—the right to contribute to your own priorities. Bureaucrats won't be able to grow government programs unless they perform well. Otherwise people won't support them with their tax dollars. Remember how you learned in school that the slogan of the American revolution was "No Taxation Without Representation"?

Ted: Yes.

Glenda: Well, we're saying No Taxation Without Manifestation. Citizens want to see their tax dollars manifest the things they want. If you pay for infrastructure, you should see new construction, fewer potholes, better bridges. If you pay for cancer research, you should see the cancer mortality rate decrease. Americans like to get things done, and to have them done right. I know you don't like big government, Ted, so this would be an opportunity to limit funding of government programs that don't produce results or are not valuable to the American people. In fact, I thought of another slogan – Taxes Without Results Are Just Insults.

Navya: I like this! Would love to allocate my tax dollars to things that promote business. Do you have a name for this new concept, Glenda?

Glenda: I call it "Vote Your Wallet."

###

As Spring approached, sap rose in trees and in the hearts of the American people. Days grew slightly longer, slightly warmer. The immediate shock of the sabotage and terrorism abated after suspects were arrested. Something inherent in the American spirit, the ineffable quality that gave the world ice cream, Barnum & Bailey, Coke, the '57 Corvette, a moon landing, the internet, and Breaking Bad – that combination of yearning, innovation and belief in a better future was palpable as it whooshed through the grassroots of America. Americans remembered a few years ago when masses of voters had felt enthusiasm for a grandfatherly socialist. Others had been drawn to the frank and politically incorrect rhetoric of a celebrity mogul. The fervor Americans had felt when they came nano-close to launching a massive bottom-up political revolution had been frustrated. And now, all of that sap was once again rising.

Into this restless Spring, Glenda and the Peeps tossed her novel proposition: that U.S. citizens, not Congress, should hold the power of the purse. The Peeps printed and distributed brochures, bumper stickers, pamphlets, and flyers. Raven, with occasional help from Vivi, pushed the concept on local TV and social media. Glenda wrote letters to the editor of every major newspaper. The subsequent antics in the House of Representatives made Fort Lauderdale's Spring break seem restrained.

And all across the country that Spring, political restlessness and civic curiosity sizzled.

Two long-retired school bus drivers tugged the levers of slot machines at a casino in the coastal town of Florence, Oregon. One hitched up her sagging knee-highs and turned to her friend. "It's about damned time, Connie. Government doesn't know how to spend money. You tell me – would a senator know how to live on social security? No way."

"I don't know, Leigh. Might be too complicated. I mean, I don't know what all these government programs are for or how much it costs to run them."

"All the more reason to let taxpayers get involved so we can learn what's going on. I tell you, Connie, it's an idea whose time has come." Leigh pulled the lever once more and heard a welcome clink-clank-bling!

Six south Philly homies sat on the stoop down the street from the fish market, smoking weed, and shootin' the shit. Jerome's cell phone beeped. He pulled it from his jacket pocket, read the screen and told his friends, "Damn, @VoteYourWallet had 240,000 followers last week. It just went over a million. Some serious shit this country's gettin' into. A friggin' revolution!"

In the commissary of the Point Loma Naval Base in San Diego, a checkout clerk covertly slipped a Vote Your Wallet brochure into every grocery bag.

The Albuquerque bowling team Salsa Spares changed their name to the Wallet Voters. They proudly had the new name embroidered on all of their team shirts.

At the Dairy Queen in Clinton, MS six mothers in their 30's treated their kids to ice cream while they talked about this Vote Your Wallet thing they'd seen on Facebook.

A car dealership in Boise, Idaho began their own "Vote Your Wallet" ad campaign in which they mocked up old income tax forms and inserted sedans, minivans, and sports car selections from their entire line as options you could 'vote' for.

In malls and bait shops and YMCAs; in coffee shops, feed stores, and on college campuses, people considered taking back the power of the purse. Citizens emailed their Senators and Congressional Reps.

Across the country that Spring, Americans remained cynical about political corruption, but somehow felt a bit more hopeful about one another. The terrorist act had given all Americans a common enemy and Vote Your Wallet gave them common cause. The only Americans who didn't sense the zeitgeist for political change sat in the hallowed halls of Congress. Had it slipped their minds that the first American Revolution was triggered by taxes?

Chapter 22

Most of America thought President Peabody launched his day with the annual White House Easter Egg Roll. After all, hundreds of little buggers held an eager, rowdy watch over the White House lawn by 6:30 a.m. But Peabody's day had actually started earlier, when the Secret Service woke him at 3:53 a.m. Moments later Peabody tucked in his shirttail and double-checked his fly, then opened the door to the Situation Room and joined the grim array of senior military officers, cabinet members, and agency heads awaiting him.

"We have two situations, Mr. President," began Director of National Intelligence David Nirvidian.

"First priority?"

"Surveillance satellites captured images of Russian troops massing on the Russia-Mongolian border. Intelligence analysts confirmed the 22nd Russian Infantry and the 43rd Russian Tank Battalions have been deployed to Mongolia."

General Franklin Ford, a 5-star who led the U. S. Army with integrity and grit, leaned toward the President. "We've seen troop movement on the southern border, too." He paused then clarified. "Chinese troops."

"Unintended consequences," Peabody murmured.

"Sir?" asked Roger Shellish.

"The troop maneuvers are the unintended consequence of switching from fracking to Fricking. Fricking's a cleaner energy source, but until all energy-generating resources are freely given by nature, like solar and wind, we'll be forced to deal with human greed. When there's high demand for gas, oil, or in the case of Fricking, copper by-products, the greedy will try to corner the market." The President turned to his Secretary of State. "What do you think, Jim?"

The Secretary answered, "We've had diplomatic relations with Mongolia for more than 25 years. We bolster their economy through USAID. I think they'll look to us for leadership."

"Any new communication from the Mongolian Ambassador?" the President asked.

"Not in the past two hours. We'll keep you posted."

President Peabody ordered the brass-encrusted players in the Sit Room to continue to monitor troop movements. He asked Roger to lean hard on the head of the UN Security Council, and to involve the National Security Advisor and the Mongolian Ambassador. He took a deep breath and inquired, "What's the other situation?"

David Nirvidian's lower lip almost went into spasm. "Mr. President, a while ago I briefed you on a homegrown militia movement of survivalists living underground in tunnels and fallout shelters. Perhaps you remember? They call themselves the 'Neath Carolina Movement."

"Yes. Mostly in North and South Carolina and Georgia, right? You thought they might be stealing arms from National Guard armories. You've been tracking them and were going to update me if they became a real threat."

208

"They've become a real threat."

"What's changed?"

"There's increasing unrest in the country, Mr. President, and that's led to more and more of these self-styled survivalists arming themselves and going underground in all senses of the word. They not only live in underground facilities; they also live "off the grid." They're difficult for us to track accurately. Our best estimates say they now have underground networks almost equal in area to the state of Delaware. We keep an eye on them, but until now they haven't been creating problems." Nirvidian paused and looked at Peabody. "Late last night several of the homeless tunnel dwellers here in D.C. alerted police to construction work going on down there. Homeland Security has known for a while that there were a few 'Neath Carolina Movement folks in the D.C. tunnels, but they didn't expect them to be living only a few hundred yards from the White House tunnels. Homeland Security believes their leader, Lester Chaffey, decided to test our limits. He's probably the one in the new underground spaces near the White House."

"So you're saying 'Neath Carolina is nearly 'Neath the White House?"

"Precisely, Mr. President."

Peabody thought for a moment, sucking down brain synapse reinforcement from a coffee cup. "Have Homeland Security clear out any of them within a five-block perimeter of the White House tunnel entrances. Warn any other 'Neath Carolina Movement members in D.C. that the party's over. Have them confiscate weapons and ammunition. I gather these folks have rather anti-social dispositions so try not to irritate them and make things worse. Cut deals; offer them

209

transportation back to wherever they came from. And find their leader and bring him in for a sit-down." Peabody stood up. "Thank you, all."

Nate Festring poured a highly audible mixture of tar and feathers, vitriol, and junk-food logic into the ear of Senator Henry Lacomb, who held his cell phone at arm's length until Festring calmed down. Festring let the Senator know in no uncertain terms that any President who let ISIS kill an entire football team without demolishing Damascus was a total pansy ass. Lacomb reminded Festring that the perpetrators had been arrested and that new anti-ISIS tactics were in process.

In the thoughtful, respectful manner in which trash-talk radio is conducted, Festring said, "If you ever wonder where your balls went, Henry, check under your petticoat."

"Not fair, Nate. I'm a Senator and the Senate's ready to do its part. What do you expect me to do? You have a bigger bully pulpit than I do!"

"Gonna use it, too. Here we sit, the most powerful nation on earth, playing tiddlywinks with these rag heads. Damn, I miss Dubya."

When Senator Lacomb returned to his office, his secretary gave him a phone message from NSA agent Tom McCorkle. McCorkle had done him favors from time to time and NSA was a good place to have friends you could tap for favors. Lacomb returned his call.

"Good news, Senator," McCorkle began.

"I could stand some good news today, Tom. What's up?"

"Remember when you asked me if NSA could figure out who hacked into all those blogs and replaced their content with that 'We're the Peeps and we're taking back our nation' crap?"

"Yes."

"Well, the hacker was ingenious. I had to pull five agents and put them to work on this exclusively for months. But the hacker finally slipped up and we were able to track the blog posts."

"Who was it?"

"A 50-something divorcée in St. Louis wrote the blog content. The hacker was a teenage girl in Texas. We haven't yet figured out how she's connected to the woman in St. Louis. Here's the juicy part – the hacker has been given immunity by the White House for her assistance in tracking ISIS communications on social media. But the one who wrote the blog content doesn't have immunity."

"Nor will she, if I have anything to do with it," Lacomb declared. "What's her name?"

"Glenda Tramboy. Our lawyers are preparing a warrant for her arrest."

###

Roger Shellish handed the President a file stamped Property of Homeland Security. "Here's the profile on Lester Chaffey, Mr. President. He's a 59-year-old ex-tobacco farmer from Reetnick, South Carolina."

"An ex-tobacco farmer? Did he switch to some less nefarious crop?"

"His farm business went under about two years ago. That's when he created this 'Neath Carolina Movement."

"When will he arrive? Maybe I can reason with him and get him to abandon this movement."

"Well, sir, that's a bit of a problem." Shellish ran his fingers through his spiky red hair. "He won't come out of his underground shelter, sir. In fact, none of them will."

"Even the ones near the White House tunnels?"

"They're still there. The FBI doesn't want to breach their bunkers by force because we think they may have booby trapped the entrances. They're trying to talk them out of the tunnels. Do you want to authorize use of force?"

"Not yet, Roger. Have them stick with non-violent strategies for now. Can we cut off electricity or water?"

"These people are survivalists, sir. They have their own generators and plenty of food and water."

"How about tossing tear gas down their ventilation holes, something like that?"

"They tried that. Apparently these survivalists also have plenty of gas masks."

"My day began in the Sit Room trying to shimmy between Russia and China. Then I smiled for the press cameras as rug rats tugged at my pant legs during the Easter Egg Roll. When I read the *Post* this morning, there was more ink about this Vote Your Wallet concept—a populist movement which I have nothing to do with. And now I can't even get a depressed ex-tobacco farmer to leave his lair!" Peabody sighed. "If, as U.S. President, I'm considered the most powerful person in the world, I hate to think of what lesser mortals have to deal with!"

Chapter 23

Raven could scarcely contain her excitement. She logged onto the Peeps chat room and messaged Glenda.

Raven: OMG!! You're not going to believe this! I've been Tweeting about Vote Your Wallet. Among my Twitter followers is a professional organization of TV producers. One of them used to work on the Daily Show before Jon Stewart left. Well, she forwarded my Vote Your Wallet Tweets to him, and he wants to interview you during the special he's doing next Weds.! I know you're the best spokesperson for the concept, Glenda, but if you decide you don't want to do this, let me know, 'cause I'd be hella jazzed to appear with Jon Stewart!

Glenda contacted Vivi immediately and asked if she could program a limited working demo of the Vote Your Wallet tax form. Fortunately the busy high school senior, camo-wearing badass Latina, hacker, and let's-make-love-in-the-lava-tubes-Icelandic-tourist reacted the way most of her contemporaries would if they had a chance to contribute to a Jon Stewart special. Vivi's demo was designed, programmed, tested and ready two days before the show. Granted, she lifted much of the content from government sites, but still...

Raven and Glenda flew to New York City. Raven helped Glenda shop for a crisp suit that would compliment her coloring on TV. After a fresh haircut and Procrustean eyebrow management, Glenda prepped for the interview. What questions would the amazing Jon Stewart ask her?

As the makeup person powdered and spritzed Glenda in the green room of the broadcast studio, Raven handed her a mild sedative and a glass of water. Glenda had already tossed her cookies twice from nerves. Time felt distorted as did her breathing –too slow, too fast, hyperventilating, holding her breath –sensations Glenda would have difficulty describing when she later related the experience to friends. Suddenly a production assistant called her name; it was time to walk onto the set and meet a man she admired.

During the first part of the show, Stewart brought The Boss on set to sing Happy Birthday to the newly appointed Supreme Court Justice. There was a commercial break, then Glenda heard, "Please welcome my next guest, Glenda Tramboy, organizer of the Vote Your Wallet movement!" Steered by a production assistant, Glenda walked on set and sat down across from her host.

Bright lights shone in her face. Stewart smiled at her and asked, "First, I'm not sure how to break this to you, but I think there's an error in your slogan. Shouldn't it be 'Vote Your Ballot'?" he teased.

Glenda smiled shyly. "No, Jon, it really is Vote Your Wallet."

"Well, if you're absolutely sure…Tell us about this idea of yours."

"It's pretty simple. When the Founding Fathers wrote the Constitution, they wanted a close and direct link between the people and the power of the purse. The House of Representatives was thought of as 'the People's house' back then, so the House was given the assignment of appropriating tax money to pay for the work of the people. Fast-forward two hundred-forty-plus years… Now, most Americans know that the House is in political gridlock and corruption has corroded the system. So Vote Your Wallet is a return to the Founding Fathers' intentions – linking the power of the purse back to the American people. We have technology that allows us to do that now; the Founding Fathers didn't."

Stewart leaned into the conversation. "Whoa! You want Americans to take the power of the purse away from Congress?"

"Yes, for all of the discretionary spending anyway. There would be certain fixed obligations the U. S. government must pay for like interest on our national debt or treaty commitments to our allies. And we exempt Social Security because people have paid into it for years; it's an investment, not an entitlement. But everything discretionary should be on the table."

Stewart looked at her with an impish grin. "Do you realize how pissed off Congress is going to be if you do this? I mean, if they can't push for tax cuts for the rich, or give away subsidies, take kick-backs or dole out sole-source contracts…" he paused, looked out at the audience, and snapped his fingers. "Oh my god, there's no reason to run for office!" When the audience laughter died down, Jon said, "I see you brought your very own Mr. Wizard demo. Ready to show us how it works?"

Glenda nodded and clicked the mouse of the laptop on the table between them. The camera crew cut to extreme close-ups of the computer screen. Over the shot, Glenda said, "OK; this is just a simplified demo, but when you file your taxes, you'd have an electronic form a lot like this one. Now, right here…" Glenda hovered the mouse above an icon labeled Last Year. "If you click here, it tells you what percentage of your tax money went to various government programs and purposes last year." She clicked the icon and the screen showed viewers a list. "Last year 51% of the tax money paid by this individual went to the military."

Stewart interjected some snark, "And 26% went for the legal defense of senators accused of chicanery?"

Caught off guard, Glenda froze.

Ever the gracious host, Stewart came to the rescue. "So, this e-form would give you the past year's tax breakdown for comparison, right?" He reached out and touched the laptop screen, pointing. "And I'm guessing this is where you type in this year's portion?"

"Right. Let's say this individual wanted to be more supportive of veterans. He or she could type in 25%, designating one quarter of their tax payment to the Department of Veterans Affairs."

"Lots of people are probably wondering – would Vote Your Wallet let you get specific? Like, if you want to pay more tax money to VA hospitals but you didn't want any of it to go to salary raises for VA bureaucrats?" Stewart asked.

Glenda picked up the mouse again and hovered over an X in a box near the words Department of Veterans Affairs. "Yes. These boxes give you expandable menus for every major government cost-center." She clicked and a long list of spending subcategories appeared. The camera followed as she demonstrated. "The government's budget is so complex that we can't show every small program or budget line-item. But tax payers would have a lot of leeway to spend their tax dollars on what they believe in."

Jon Stewart rubbed his hands together and laughed. "I won't have to fund Dick Cheney's Secret Service detail anymore! Hot damn! I'm likin' this idea!" Stewart switched to a more serious tone. "So, if this Vote Your Wallet legislation were to pass, how would federal agencies and departments budget for their expenses?"

Glenda responded, "It would have to be phased in gradually over a number of years. Perhaps the first year could be a dry run, just to let citizens know what the budget they created would look like." Her throat was dry from nervousness. She reached for the glass of water on the table and took a long swallow. "Then maybe the second year, people would get to allocate, say, 10% of their total tax dollars. And maybe the following year, 30%. And so on, until the people had 100% of the power of the purse for all discretionary spending. Now, that's empowered democracy!"

"Sounds to me," Steward mused, "that over time, Vote Your Wallet would decrease the power and influence of political parties. They'd have fewer ways to scare or cajole us with fundraising emails."

"And maybe that's a good thing."

"Congress is not going to like this <u>at all</u>," Jon remarked. "How do you propose to get this passed? I'm just spit-balling here, but I'm thinking maybe fill the Capitol building with nitrous oxide?"

"The only way is for citizens to demand it. That means thousands of letters and phone calls to Congress. And marches, demonstrations, rallies…" Glenda's eyes gleamed and her cheeks flushed with color. "Many of you joined grassroots movements in 2015 and 2016 —you were enthused because democracy made your heart race; you felt you had a voice. Well, you have a voice --and a choice -- now. Vote Your Wallet will lead a march on Washington next week on tax day, April 15th. We'll gather at noon at the IRS building and march from there onto the Washington Mall." Glenda turned from Jon Stewart and looked directly into Camera #5 as Raven had suggested. "We need you --- every one of you – to participate. Call your Congressional Rep, and come march with us for Vote Your Wallet!"

Stewart swung his chair and faced Camera #5, too. "Glenda Tramboy of the Vote Your Wallet movement! Thank you for joining us." He reached across the table and shook Glenda's hand. She'd been interviewed by Jon Stewart! Somehow all of her online dating misadventures paled by comparison.

"Coming up in the next half of the show: The Loen Brothers will share insights into their new film, *Gimme Gravy*, about the creators of edible underwear. Stay tuned."

Raven got to meet Stewart backstage for a few minutes. Both women understood what a PR coup they'd just pulled off. Stewart's return to the small screen with this network special drew almost as many viewers as a World Series game or major Olympic event. The word was out!

###

April 15th spread over Washington, D.C. like a pink and white blessing. Three thousand Japanese cherry trees were in bloom and the weather had been downloaded from nirvana. The National Cherry Blossom Festival had ended a few days earlier, but the blossoms didn't know that. They persisted in sprinkling magic up and down the Washington Mall.

The Peeps arrived early to finalize permits, stage sound equipment, and set up a canopy. Vivi invited Einar who made his first trip to the U.S. to attend the rally. Raven's fiancé Will, now stationed at the Pentagon, joined them. Ted brought his girlfriend Sherry. DeVille invited the co-owner of his restaurant. Navya's husband had finally realized his wife was more interesting than tonsils and he stood on the stage with her, meeting and greeting the others. Emery and Matt had flown out together, meeting up with Emery's brother, the Constitutional lawyer, who also joined them. Perhaps the biggest surprise was that Sarantha slipped the scrutiny of her Secret Service agents to stand with the Peeps. Even though Vote Your Wallet wasn't personally meaningful to a girl who'd never paid a dollar of income tax in her life, she could feel the energy of the crowd. Something big was going on in America and she felt part of it.

People from across the nation arrived, too, by bus, bicycle, Metro, and taxi. Thousands left offices, classrooms, restaurants, or shops to join the movement. Every imaginable race, ethnicity, age and background showed an interest in Vote Your Wallet. The Tea Party, liberals, Mormons, Muslims, Evangelicals, transgendered folks, Amway sales people, 12-Step groups – everyone –liked the idea of taking the power of the purse back from Congress. Everyone except the 535 members of that venerable institution, that is.

At noon the masses blocked the streets in both directions at the I.R.S. headquarters building on the corner of Constitution Avenue and 12th. Traffic barricades rerouted anyone foolish enough to drive in this crowd. The sea of humans grew to tidal wave proportions which might have been alarming if the sky hadn't been baby blue and the air hadn't been perfumed with cherry blossoms. Throughout the crowd people held high Vote Your Wallet and No Taxation Without Manifestation signs. Parents carried toddlers on their shoulders. Some folks on the perimeters of the crowd flew kites. It was just that kind of day.

Glenda and DeVille walked up the steps of the IRS building carrying a cardboard box. Glenda had asked DeVille to help her mainly because his size offered some protection. They opened the door and demanded to see the Commissioner of IRS. Realizing how many media cameras and cell phones would record the moment, the Commissioner met with them. She was pleasant and businesslike as Glenda and DeVille officially delivered the box containing written justification and full design of their Vote Your Wallet program, including the software code for the new tax form. The Commissioner could afford to be gracious; she held no power whatsoever over whether Congress would approve the idea.

Glenda and DeVille returned to the others and led the march down 12th, around the Smithsonian, out onto the National Mall, and all the way to their staging area. The afternoon sun grew warmer. The Peeps climbed onto the stage. They kept looking at one another as if to say, 'Did we really do this?'

Glenda stepped up to the mike. She stood there for a moment gazing over the crowd, taking in both the diversity and immensity of America. Then she took a deep breath that drew from her heart, and began.

"You think Congress is getting the message?" She yelled, spreading her arms, gesturing at the vibrant democracy in front of her. "Well, we're sending them a message! Vote Your Wallet!"

The crowd began to chant back an echo: Vote Your Wallet! Vote Your Wallet!

Glenda began again in a soft voice so the crowd had to quiet to hear her. "Vote Your Wallet is an idea whose time has come. Americans come up with a lot of good ideas, things like public education or equal rights for all. Sometimes we take two steps forward and one step back. But we persist, and then a new idea surfaces that makes us a stronger, freer people.

"America is exceptional precisely because we welcome people from all backgrounds, classes, and nations to build this country. Such an incredible variety of people guarantees variety in the way people perceive and understand the world. America excels at innovation, invention, and entertainment precisely because of our multicultural democracy; because our sense of who we are has never limited who we might become.

"We're living in a time now when our democracy needs our help.

"You've probably all heard the story about how to boil a frog. You first put the frog into a pot of cool water, then you turn on the burner under the pot. The cool water becomes tepid, then soothing warm water.... which gets hotter. Soon the water is boiling and the frog is cooked.

"Little by little. One step at a time. That's how it happens when a democracy transitions into a plutocracy – a nation ruled by the wealthy. We say we're a democracy, a government of the people, by the people, and for the people. But would a democratic government pass a piece of

222

legislation that *98% of its citizens* disapproved of? That's what Congress did when it passed Section 1021 of the National Defense Authorization Act which says the military can seize a U.S. citizen and hold them indefinitely without due process. Sound unconstitutional? That's because it is! And 98% of the people polled said they disagreed with it. Yet your Congress passed that into law.

"And what about all of the things that you wish Congress would pass but don't because lobbyists and other power brokers inevitably get in the way?

"Yes, it's time to check the temperature of the water in the pot before our democracy is cooked! Vote Your Wallet will help with that.

"Vote Your Wallet is a big step forward. It's a start. But it won't fix everything. There are other factors weakening our democracy, like the decreasing educational level of our citizens, the profit-orientation of our news media, and our own human character flaws."

A sudden breeze floated a raft of cherry petals over the stage where it hovered momentarily, lending a hypnotic effect.

Glenda paused; the crowd was more subdued. People don't like to be scolded. She had to handle this adeptly. "Maybe this all sounds too hard. Maybe you're thinking to yourself, 'I don't have time to follow everything Congress does. I don't have time to write to my representatives. I don't have time to read all that election literature. I don't have time to serve on jury duty or a civic committee.

"Well, here's the hard truth: No one's going to make you. In fact, you are not wanted! The 1% who pull the puppet strings of power will continue to provide you distractions and excitement—all kinds of shtick. They'll do almost anything except let you handle the puppet strings. America is on its way to becoming a second-class nation if we don't fix our infrastructure, educate our citizens, and address the residual problems of racism.

"So, yes, we can continue to be apathetic.

"Or …instead of seeing government as either the enemy or as the solution to every societal problem, we can begin to see government as a hub for connecting businesses and non-profits to the people. We can get more involved in co-ops, credit unions, consortiums…"

From the back of the stage, murmurs grew into wary shouts from the crowd. A cadre of roughly 30 FBI officers wearing Riot Control gear made a steady incursion into the crowd and approached the stage. They climbed onto the platform and headed for Glenda. She was still speaking when one of the officers took her by the upper arm and said, "Glenda Tramboy, you are under arrest as a co-conspirator in computer crimes and for treason against your government. You have the right to remain silent. You have the right to an attorney. If you cannot afford an attorney, one will be appointed for you."

As she was taken away, she managed to yell, "You cannot arrest an idea!"

The lead FBI agent signaled his fellow troops who created a protective formation with Glenda in the center. They began slowly moving through the crowd toward a waiting FBI van near the traffic barricade.

Suddenly an even larger, well-equipped cadre of National Guard soldiers approached from 12th Street. The officer in charge consulted with the lead FBI agent of the first group and handed them some paperwork. In response, the first group turned Glenda over to the second. Soon the National Guard troops mounted the stage, asked everyone standing there for ID, and arrested all of the other Peeps, including Sarantha.

This time, even cherry blossoms couldn't make it a pretty picture.

Chapter 24

When Glenda, Vivi, Emery, Raven, Navya, DeVille, Ted, and Sarantha were apprehended, they were hustled into a large military van. Hoods were placed over their heads. After some initial ineffective bluster, the Peeps didn't say much. Each seemed to be trying to catch any clue, locate any piece of the puzzle as to what the hell was happening.

After a high-anxiety ten-minute slog circumventing people and barricades, the van stopped and the Peeps were helped out. Still wearing hoods, they were escorted somewhere. The only info they could gather was that it was a hard surface under their feet that didn't feel like brick or gravel, and by dint of the short drive, they were probably still in D.C.

Their captors navigated them through twists and turns. They then went on some kind of elevator and heard beeps and buzzers as doors opened on different levels. More doors closed behind them. The soldiers continued to steer them through some kind of corridor. The ground beneath their feet felt like tile. Another set of doors opened. Finally, the Peeps entered another room and one by one, their hoods were removed.

In front of them a breathtaking, arched Tiffany paned glass window played with the sunshine of the April afternoon. The Peeps found themselves in the West Sitting Hall of the White House Residence, an airy, dramatic room Eleanor Roosevelt had enjoyed. President Peabody was in the room along with a handful of others. When Sarantha saw her father, she ran over to him. He wrapped his arms around her in relief.

Peabody released Sarantha and addressed them. "Welcome, Peeps! That's what you call yourselves, right? Peeps? You obviously know who I am. Let me introduce the others. This is Roger Shellish, my Chief of Staff."

Roger nodded his head in greeting toward these people he'd heard and read so much about. He felt something unique course through him when he met Glenda in person. He'd caught her appearance with Jon Stewart, and had been left with an impression of sharp intelligence and deep awareness. Her skin was flushed both from the April sunshine and from her passion at the rally.

The President then turned to Mohiinok, who sat cross-legged on the floor in a corner of the room, loading a long ceremonial pipe. "This is my great-uncle Mohiinok, elder shaman of the Winooku tribe. He's my great-grand-mother's brother and, as I've come to appreciate, a very wise soul. Through an intertribal network of Native Americans across the country, Mohiinok has been tracking all of you to be sure you and my daughter were safe."

Murmurs of "that explains a few things!" and "Oh, I wondered how…" buzzed around the room. Most of the Peeps now wore sheepish grins. But what the heck were they doing at the White House? What did the President have in mind?

Sarantha sat down on the floor near her great-uncle Mohiinok, imitating his cross-legged position. He winked and grinned at her.

President Peabody continued in a warm, respectful tone, "Mohiinok and I have spent considerable time together

227

in the past few days. He has been helpful to me regarding our current situation. More about that later." Peabody turned his attention to Demmy. "And this beautiful woman is Dr. Demetra Phillips, Sarantha's mother and my favorite doctor without a border." His manner shifted from flirtatious to concern. "By the way, do any of you need medical attention?" He let the question hang in the air; none of the Peeps seemed worse for the wear.

"I've had a few heart problems and…" DeVille seemed short of breath. He recited, "Fu jingle mingle tingle. If you happen to have a stethoscope handy, I'd like to know how my old ticker is doing," he said. Demmy went for her medical bag.

Navya summoned the courage to speak up. "Mr. President, my husband is also a physician. He was with me at the rally. We all had friends and family with us at the march. Do we know if they're safe? Have they been arrested?"

Peabody picked up a phone and called his executive secretary. "Can you meet me in the Residence? I'm in the West Sitting Hall. Thanks." He looked at the people around him. "If you'll give my secretary the name and phone number of the person or persons you're looking for, I'll have her contact them, let them know you're OK. And we'll make sure they're OK." The Peeps quickly wrote down contact info for their loved ones.

Demmy pronounced DeVille stable, if a little winded, after their adventure with the police.

Glenda spoke up. "Well, if no one else is going to ask, I will. What the heck's going on? Why were we arrested? Are we going to be held in the White House?"

President Peabody opened his mouth to begin an answer, but his cell phone rang. He glanced down at the cell screen, saw that the call demanded his attention, and excused himself. He walked out into the corridor to talk, leaving Roger Shellish in charge.

When he returned, he seemed quite upbeat. He approached Roger who sat on an overstuffed chair. "That was Nirvidian. The UN Security Council met today on the Mongolian situation. They're sending a UN Preventive Deployment Force to Mongolia. Nirvidian's optimistic they'll work something out."

"Candidly, Mr. President, I'm surprised," remarked Roger. "Apparently my opinion of the usefulness of the United Nations in international conflicts was less than it should have been."

"Normally they're a useless pack of fawning, feckless diplomats who couldn't tie their own shoes without six meetings and a committee report. But I thought the U.N. Security Council was a good bet this time. China and Russia are permanent members, so they'd try to out-do one another in appearing cooperative on the world stage. And Ukraine and Japan are two of the temporary members. You know what Poroshenko thinks of Putin! I figured Ukraine would make a lot of noise if Russia didn't cooperate, and Japan would lean on China. It was worth a shot."

Peabody's secretary entered the room. She took the Peeps' contact info for friends and family. The President also asked her to have a variety of food and drinks delivered to the Residence. He then turned back to the Peeps, and in particular, Glenda. "I'm sorry we were interrupted. Now, you wanted to know…"

"Why were we arrested? Or were we? What are we doing here? There were about 40,000 thousand Americans on the Washington Mall this afternoon who had their hopes up about building a better democracy. Are they still out there?" Her eyes went to the semi-circular window to scan the distance for signs of the crowd.

"As far as the rally goes, the D.C. police have been told to make sure activities remain non-violent but otherwise not to interfere. I hope every single person there marches to Capitol Hill and screams Vote Your Wallet in every Congressional ear! And yes, you, Ms. Tramboy, were arrested. Senator Lacomb – you know who he is?" the President asked.

"Oh, yes." The tone of Glenda's voice made clear her opinion of the Senator.

"Well, Lacomb has a contact in the NSA. He brought pressure on his NSA pal to identify the source of the blog-hack last summer. It took them months, but they identified Vivi here." Peabody glanced over at Vivi, who seemed quite comfortable being in the same room as the President of the United States. "Vivi's helped us with cyber counter-terrorism efforts. She's brought several of her ha..." The President started to say 'hacker' but changed his mind. "...computer savvy friends into the task force, too. Because of her efforts, I granted Vivi, along with some of her friends, immunity from any computer crimes they might be accused of. But through Vivi they found you, Glenda, and you didn't have immunity."

The President continued. "So, yes, you were arrested. As soon as I heard about the arrest warrant, I knew they'd find your online chat room and all hell would break loose. They'd see that Sarantha was involved in the Peeps--

230

just the kind of political leverage Lacomb would love to have on me. So I deployed the National Guard to bring all of you into protective custody."

"I guess we owe you a thank you," said Ted, "but why did you have to put hoods over our heads? Why scare the crap out of us, pardon my language?"

"Had to," answered Peabody. "You were routed through special White House security tunnels so no one would know where you were. The locations of those security entrances and exits are Top Secret. I would have broken the law if I'd let you see where you were going."

"Speaking of underground tunnels, sir..." Roger verbally nudged the President.

"Damn, we still haven't gotten them out of there?"

"No, sir."

"You still haven't gotten who out of where?" Raven's reporter curiosity quickened.

President Peabody and Roger took turns filling the Peeps in on the 'Neath Carolina Movement situation.

"I have idea. Would work." This from Mohiinok, in a throaty whisper.

"It's not a simple task, Uncle. We've tried all kinds of things. Without doing something cruel, I don't know how to get them out of there."

Again. "I have idea. Would work." Then Mohiinok stood up, wobbled a bit, steadied himself, walked over to Peabody, and whispered in his ear.

A delicious grin split Peabody's face. "Definitely worth a try!" The President made a call ordering the purchase of millions of no-see-ums and chiggers to be dumped into the 'Neath Carolina bunkers' ventilation system. The entomology vendor, one who provided insects for many a National Institutes of Health contract, promised delivery within 48 hours.

Peabody's secretary had an assortment of sandwiches, salads and beverages brought to the West Sitting Hall. Emery offered a short grace. The group ate, drank, and chatted, trying to absorb everything that had happened, everything they'd learned, in the past few hours.

President Peabody went to sit near Demmy and quietly thanked her for coming.

Demmy scanned and saw that Sarantha was on the opposite side of the room discussing the Open Source philosophy with Vivi. "Our daughter was in danger, Sam. Of course I came."

"After your Christmas visit…well, I've given a lot of thought to what can and can't be done to improve our government." He looked her in the eyes, fanning that old familiar spark; blowing on the one remaining ember. "I've decided to do something…" he chose the word carefully, "extraordinary. Hang out with us for a few days; you'll see."

Demmy didn't comment but he knew he'd caught her interest.

Glenda asked, "What's our legal status now? Are we free to go home?"

President Peabody turned his considerable charm back to Glenda. "If you're not content with my hospitality,

I'm not going to fight you. I'll issue papers granting you immunity, and you can leave. However, we're about to embark on a major experiment in American government. You especially, Ms. Tramboy, might want to stick around."

"When will this 'experiment in American government' start?"

"At sunset tonight."

Sunlight streaming through the half-moon window began to fade, melting a warm butterscotch color over the walls. Sunset wouldn't be long now.

"There's a TV in the Treaty Room down the hall," said the President. "Let's see what's going on with the rally." He and Roger led the group there and turned on CNN. They watched with hope as thousands of Vote Your Wallet demonstrators swarmed around the Capitol building.

"Finally," said Glenda, "...after so many populist movements, the voice of the people sounds a clarion call that Congress can't ignore!"

"Ms. Tramboy..." Roger began.

"Please, call me Glenda."

"Glenda, I just want to say how much I admire your concept of democracy. If only more people felt like you do." It felt awkward to Roger to compliment a woman he barely knew, but he meant it. This woman stirred something in him that hadn't been stirred, shaken, or poured over ice in a long, long time.

The President checked his watch. "Roger, would you mind showing everyone the rest of the Residence? I have some things to attend to." President Peabody signaled Mohiinok, who stood and followed him out.

Roger gathered the group and led them on an informal mini-tour of the White House Residence. They were seeing rooms few people ever saw.

About half an hour before sunset, President Peabody's limo driver took him and Mohiinok to the Embassy of Tribal Nations on P Street.

Peabody and Mohiinok were greeted by a large council of tribal leaders. They weren't exactly rude to Peabody, but it was clear they had more respect for Mohiinok than for some white guy who'd lucked his way into the Presidency. Peabody thanked them profusely for their assistance in keeping an eye on Sarantha and ensuring her safety.

They were there to sign a document appointing Basho Samuels Peabody of the Ojibwa tribe as Chieftain of the Great Council of Native American Tribal Leaders-- the closest thing to an officially designated leader of all U. S. Native Americans as anyone could be. The document was signed by all parties exactly at sundown. After sharing a peace pipe with the tribal leaders, Peabody signed another document as Chieftain on behalf of the Great Council—a Declaration of War against the United States of America for broken treaties. The council members and Peabody chatted for a few minutes, then Peabody and Mohiinok returned to the limo.

234

On the drive back to the White House, Peabody said to Mohiinok, "I hope I did the right thing, Uncle. It feels a little intimidating to declare war on one's own country. If things don't go well… if the people don't support what I'm trying to do..." He let the potential repercussions hang in the air.

When they returned to the Residence, they found Roger Shellish and Glenda, heads together, deep in conversation sipping tea in the living room. Emery had excused himself and gone into the sitting room off the Lincoln Bedroom to pray for the Peeps and the country they all believed in. DeVille and Ted were leapfrogging black and red checkers across a game board. Raven, Demmy and Navya chatted in the Treaty Room. Out on the Truman balcony, Vivi showed Sarantha video clips of her boyfriend Einar.

President Peabody gathered them all together again in the Residence dining room. "I can't explain everything yet, but I would appreciate it if you'd agree to remain in the White House as my guests for the next three days until April 18th. I will be in and out; I need to attend to the business of the country and will spend some time here, but mostly I'll work out of the Oval Office. My Chief of Staff, Roger, and my secretary will accommodate your needs. I think I've figured out a way to reboot the government of the United States of America. It's going to happen on the morning of the 18th. I invite you all to be present for that historic moment." The President looked around at the shocked faces surrounding him. "Meanwhile, there's no reason you can't consider this a mini-holiday. There'll be good food, we have decent wine and liquor at the White House, and whatever Mohiinok has in that pipe of his, he always seems willing to share!" He rolled his eyes and chuckled. "No, I don't inhale, not much anyway."

The President continued, "Your loved ones have been contacted; they're safe and they know you're all right. You can wander among the bedrooms, sitting rooms and offices in the Residence until you find a place to sleep that works for you. I'll stay in the Master Bedroom. You don't want to sleep there. Whenever something dreadful happens in the world, a Secret Service agent wakes you up in the middle of the night and drags you into the Situation Room."

Peabody walked over to Demmy and whispered in her ear. "In spite of that... I'd really appreciate it if you'd join me in the Master Bedroom."

Demmy reached up and took his hand in hers.

For three days the Peeps filled the White House Residence. They learned their way around the Residence kitchen and discovered which rooms had TVs. Navya took selfies in the Lincoln Bedroom, promising she wouldn't email or post them to relatives in Mumbai until their location was no longer secret. Mentally she noted she'd worked deals with properties that were more luxurious, but after all, the White House had a certain panache.

During the days, the President and Roger Shellish stayed unusually busy. Evenings were fun. They would all gather to watch TV or a movie, talk politics, play cards, etc. The President asked about their backgrounds, families, and work. He especially loved the tale of how they all met in the TSA Holding Area at Logan Airport.

Later in the evenings, Mohiinok would fire up the peace pipe and pass it around which certainly made Charades funnier. The President saw his daughter laugh for the first time in years. One night the shaman was hanging out in the President's Master Bedroom which featured a mural of songbirds in mid-flight. Mohiinok had indulged in the peace pipe before entering the room and it took him a while to realize the birds weren't real and they weren't flying. By the third night together, it felt like one big dorm party. Seven ordinary Americans discovered they actually liked their President.

Glenda Tramboy and Roger Shellish never saw it coming. He was seven years younger than she, yes. She was an odd history buff, yes. He hadn't dated since his wife died and was out of practice, yes. But she thought his spikey hair was adorable; he felt the allure of her trim body. She loved his non-egotistical way of wielding power in the White House. He loved her depth and perspicacity. The outside world may have deemed them a nerdy couple, but somehow they complemented one another. The others gave them privacy at bedtime.

President Peabody went about his business, adhering to his usual schedule in the Oval Office. He took two meetings with the House Majority Leader on Vote Your Wallet. He hosted a White House dinner for President Park of South Korea. For the first time since he'd been elected, Demmy served at his side as First Hostess. As a true global citizen, she wore the role well. Peabody directed Press Secretary Fondew to alert the media to a major news announcement scheduled for noon on April 18th.

He made the announcement from the Rose Garden which was gum-dropped with the tulips and jonquils of Spring. When President Peabody and Roger Shellish entered the stage, a line of about thirty solemn tribal council leaders in full ceremonial regalia greeted them. They worked the line, introducing themselves.

"Chief Wahchinksapa of the Sioux tribe."

"Chief Lonan of the Zuni."

"Chief… of Staff," responded Roger as he reached out to shake hands.

Mohiinok, Demmy, Sarantha and the Peeps also shared the stage, though when Mohiinok got tired of standing, he sat down in one corner of the platform. The media had been alerted; there was no shortage of cameras or reporters.

President Peabody began. "In 1988, our government passed Concurrent Resolution 331 which recognized the influence of the Iroquois Constitution over our own Constitution and Bill of Rights. The Iroquois Constitution offered freedom of religion, freedom of speech and separation of the powers in government. It was much like our own Constitution except the Iroquois included women and non-whites.

"Ironically the government that passed that resolution in 1988 barely still exists. What we now call Congress is, not in all cases, but in too many cases, dysfunctional and corrupt. Congress has written its own rules, some of which are antithetical to the spirit of the Constitution. Congress has written its own pension plan, its own salary raises and its own work schedule. They have not scheduled one 5-day work week for themselves for the foreseeable future. The American people now give Congress a 9% approval rating.

"If we are to continue to not only survive but thrive as a democratic republic, we need a government that works for the majority of its citizens. It's that simple.

"I've pondered long and hard whether there was anything I could do, realistically, to make things better. I'm just one person; can one person make a difference?" He paused again then added, "Fortunately I also asked my great uncle Mohiinok, shaman of the Winootku tribe.

"He told me an interesting story he'd heard from an elderly Jewish rabbi." President Peabody shifted the tone of his voice into storytelling mode.

"A dying father leaves 17 camels to his three sons. He wants his eldest son to have half of them, his middle son one-third, and his youngest son, one-ninth. When he dies, the sons can't decide how to divide 17 by 2, 3 or 9. They ask a village elder what to do. The elder loans them a camel, so then they have 18. They divide 18 camels by half and give nine to the eldest son. They divide 18 by three and give six camels to the middle son. They divide 18 camels by nine and give the youngest son two camels. Nine camels plus six camels plus two camels equals seventeen camels. Then they returned the last camel to the village elder."

Peabody looked up at the media cameras, pausing for dramatic effect. "In Mohiinok's tale, the village elder's camel played two roles. That camel was part of the inherited group of camels and not part of them, at the same time. Thinking about that opened possibilities.

On April 15th at sunset, I, Basho Samuels Peabody, was officially appointed Chieftain of the Great Council of Native American Tribal Leaders. As such I became the designated leader of all U. S. Native Americans.

And as their leader, I began to think about the endless treaties the American government made with indigenous peoples, and then broke them. I felt the anger and frustration of thousands of betrayals. I felt in my heart the tremendous loss of lives and desecration of the earth. And I declared war on the United States of America."

Peabody checked the crowd to see if they were tracking what he said. With the slightest hint of humor in his voice, he continued. "Then, in my role as President and Commander in Chief of the United States of America, I surrendered to the Great Council of Native American Tribal Leaders.

"Native Americans have served this country proudly in the military. They've graciously shared their wisdom and culture to help their fellow Americans. Native Americans do not want to see this country fail.

"So the tribal leaders met with me for many hours, deciding what to do with the U. S. We decided that the structural problems had become so embedded in government institutions that the only way to improve the government significantly was to do a reboot.

"Yes, reboot it, like you do your laptop.

"We, the People need a fresh start. We need a government that honors the will of its citizens, a government that hears their cries.

"We need a government that has amended its Constitution to overturn the Citizens United decision, putting elections on a more even playing field.

"We need a government that mandates both the House and Senate to introduce a bill reflecting the principles of the Vote Your Wallet movement.

"We need a government that mandates the Senate to introduce and vote on the bill known as Make Regulation Make Sense-- the bill that inspired a young man to drape the Statue of Liberty with red tape to help publicize the need to eliminate ridiculous and duplicative regulations.

"We need a government that has enacted into law the following policies because they are supported by more than two-thirds of its citizens:

- No death penalty executions unless DNA evidence proves guilt
- Allow the government   health programs to negotiate drug prices
- Immigration reform with a legal pathway to citizenship; the Great Council recommends the Palmyra-Redding Bill
- English as the official language of the United States
- Require the NSA to obtai n warrants for surveillance
- End gerrymandering   by redrawing Congressional districts through an independent, non-partisan committee
- Offer students the same low interest on loans that banks get
- Background checks on purchasers of any type of firearm
- A ban on   sales of any assault weapons
- Substantial   government investment in wind and solar energy
- S tringent limits on carbon emissions from coal plants
- Decriminalization of marijuana.

"And it's not only up to politicians and elected representatives to give us good government. We have to take it. A government that strives for an empowered democracy is one in which citizens do their fair share by staying informed, voting, serving on juries, and performing other civic duties.

"As of this moment, the Native Americans to whom we have officially surrendered will return our nation to us... with that newly rebooted, more truly democratic government I just described. Yes, you heard me correctly. As Chieftain of the Great Council, I've forced these needed changes. At sunset the Council and I will sign a new set of documents. They will return the United States back to its people. And I will step down as Chieftain of the Great Council.

"I believe the American people deserve this reboot; this new opportunity will make ours the world's greatest democracy.

"I asked the Great Council if they would like anything in return for helping America return to the kind of government the people want. The Council asked only this." Here Peabody took a piece of paper from his inside coat pocket and read directly from the note. "They asked that I remind you: 'Care for your family. Meet your neighbors. Get involved in your community. Put down your cell phone and look at the person sitting next to you. Help each other. Government cannot solve all of your problems. And at night, gaze at the stars and ponder the Great Spirit who connects us all.' Their request seems more than fair to me, since they have agreed to give us back our country—a deal we never offered them.

"If Americans would prefer to stick with the government we've had lately, let me know, and I will negate the documents and treaties signed with the Great Council these past few days. We've accrued many broken treaties in our past. If we want to continue to do that, we can.

"But I hope Americans will understand the value of a government reboot; how I have tried to be an 18th camel. I hope Americans will give themselves and our democracy a second chance.

" God bless you and God bless America."

The media were stunned. The nation was stunned. The ceremonial garb was stunning. Dr. Demetra Phillips had tears in her eyes. So did Glenda. Even Mohiinok's eyes glistened.

President Peabody signed the 'reboot' documents in the Treaty Room of the White House Residence. The White House threw quite the party afterward!

Peabody had not been as forthcoming about the pardons he'd issued to all of the Peeps and his daughter, but most Americans were understanding when they found out.

The next day the President, Demmy, Roger, and the Peeps waited to see whether emails of support or protest would pour in from the American people. By noon two White House servers had crashed with overwhelmingly positive emails. By mid-afternoon, masses of people marched on Congress –not the White House.

At sunset the Peeps and company hung out on the Truman Balcony to watch the sun go down. From the balcony they could see that about half a block away, a manhole cover was being raised. Out from an underground tunnel climbed Lester Chaffey of the 'Neath Carolina Movement. In dirty long-johns, he scratched and swatted at his arms and legs. Mohiinok's suggestion had worked!

We're the Peeps and we've cut all puppet strings!

And why not? We don't believe in puppetry. We believe in democracy.

We believe in the cantankerous tunnel dweller who feels alienated from society. We believe in dignified tribal leaders in ceremonial garb; in ordinary citizens who might create a revolution (or at least a reboot); in teenagers who will inherit both the problems and the blessings of empowered democracy. We believe in combat veterans and community organizers; in entrepreneurs and refugees – in these and millions of others.

The open secret of America is that, even when the economy falters, even when we're not certain of solutions, even in the face of terrorism, we place the sacred trust of government in the hands of friends and neighbors, and yes, even people on the other side of town.

May we always be worthy.

THE END

AUTHOR'S NOTE

The author hopes you enjoyed the political wish-fulfillment offered by *We the Peeps*. We all need imagination, fun and the inspiration of outside-the-box thinking. If you'd also like to do something on a practical level, please mail or email the following page to your Senators and Representatives.

For book readers --- Simply copy the "Issues" page, add your name and address and mail it to Congress. Consider making a few copies for friends, too.

For e-book readers --- If your e-Reader allows you to select text and copy it, copy the Issues page, then paste the text into your personal email and sent it to Congress.

ISSUES

Dear Member of Congress:

I support the following policies, as do more than two-thirds of U.S. citizens in recent polls. We are supposed to be a democracy. When you consider legislation, vote accordingly!

- No death penalty executions unless DNA evidence proves the accused is guilty
- Allow the government to negotiate drug prices
- Immigration reform with a legal pathway to citizenship
- English as the official language of the United States
- Require the NSA to obtain warrants for surveillance
- End gerrymandering and institute fair, functional redistricting
- Offer students the same low interest on loans as banks get
- Background checks on purc   hasers of any type of firearm
- A ban on sales of any assault weapons
- Substantial government investment in wind and solar energy
- Stringent limits on carbon emissions from coal plants
- Decriminalization of marijuana.

_____

Name of Citizen

_____

Address of Citizen

_____

Address of Citizen

ABOUT THE AUTHOR

Morgan Hunt was born and raised on a New Jersey barrier island. Though she's been a resident of the theater-oriented southern Oregon town of Ashland for over a decade, her writing retains a Jersey candor that punctures the pretentious. She writes in varied arenas: mystery novels, poetry, screenplays, articles and short stories. Her traditionally published Tess Camillo mystery series won a Best Books Award (USA Book News) and a National Indie Excellence Award (Independent Booksellers). Hunt's poems have been published in the *California Quarterly, San Diego Mensan,* and *Oregon State Poetry Association* chapbooks. Her article on the use of profanity in fiction appeared in *Writer's Digest.* Hunt's short story, "The Answer Box," was a Finalist in the 2014 *Saturday Evening Post* Great American Fiction contest. *We the Peeps* is her first political novel.